No Exit

A Collection of Utah Horror

Timber Ghost Press

No Exit: A Collection of Utah Horror

Published by Timber Ghost Press

Printed in the United States of America

Edited by: Beverly Bernard

Cover Art and Design by: Don Noble

Interior Design: Timber Ghost Press

Print ISBN: 979-8-9925767-1-9

www.TimberGhostPress.com

Contents

The Rite

David McLachlan

They were forty miles south of Zion when John first saw the flaming elk.

He had packed early. Got the motorhome on the road while it was still dark. Ellie and Erik were above him in the overhead sleeper. Stacy, his wife, slept in the seat next to him, her bare feet on the dash, sore ankle draped with an icepack. They had only spent two days in Zion. Not enough time really. But they got in most of the hikes John wanted then got some swag from the gift shop—John a hat, Stacy a shirt, Ellie a hoodie, and Erik a stuffed bear dressed as a park ranger.

Yes, all told, it was a successful leg of the trip so far, the highlight for John being the hike into the The Narrows with his daughter Ellie. It might have been the highlight of the whole trip so far. Sitting on the rocks, exhausted, seeing the sunlight pierce down into that impossibly deep canyon, there was something magical about being there. And seeing Ellie gaze up along those sheer cliff walls, seeing the wonder in her face, made all of the expense and effort worth it. It had been too long since John saw a smile that wide on her El's face. Much too—

He pressed hard on the brakes, leaning forward. The elk was standing there in the middle of the road, gazing indifferently at him. He fought the instinct to yank on the wheel. It was too top heavy, awkward. He'd risk dumping it in the road or in the ditch. He could only watch as the motorhome careened towards the animal, noting dumbly how the elk seemed on fire, its antlers rising up into the reddened sky like a crown of flames.

He steadied himself, preparing for impact.

And then the elk was gone.

The motorhome glided to a stop. It sat there puttering in the middle of the road. No one was coming in either direction.

Jake, their beagle, was looking at him curiously, wondering if it was time to get out and hike a leg against a bush.

"Not yet, old man," John said, laying his hand on the dog's neck.

"What is it?" Stacy said, stretching, looking around, getting her bearings.

"Something in the road," John said. He grabbed his jacket and hopped out.

Wind pulled at his hat. The cold hit him like a fist. There was no elk along the road, none trotting off in the distance. Certainly, none with flames rippling off its head and antlers like he had seen. He walked around, checked each side of the vehicle, then feeling anxious, got down and checked underneath.

Stupid, he said to himself, wiping away the asphalt pebbles that stuck to his palms. Well, you didn't run over the old boy at least.

But how could that be? It was impossible not to have run it down. Yet, there was nothing out there. He could see for miles and miles through the vast desert. He thought again of the way the bull elk stared at him. He didn't know why, but he wanted to push the image away, out of his mind.

The mountains spread out before him like a painting. The drive itself, he came to realize, was half the splendor of this trip. His family slept most of the drive, and he took pleasure in ferrying them from one adventure to the next. He felt it was his fatherly duty. And it gave time to enjoy the grandeur. Each mile told some vast geological story. Millions of years unfolded before him as he puttered along the desert highway.

Yet now, all pleasure from the landscape was gone. Out here, along the road in the middle of the desert, he felt isolated, watched. Like the way a rat must feel with the owl in the branch above.

He climbed back into the motorhome, his hands shaking as he threw it into gear.

Stacy was already in the back, brewing a batch of coffee.

A young man in a parka, with long hair blowing in the wind, leaned out of the booth as the motorhome rolled up to the entrance of the Coral Pink Sand Dunes. The man yelled out to John through the icy wind and asked if he wanted to rent a sandboard.

John wasn't sure what that was, but he was pretty sure he didn't want to. Not in this weather.

The man took John's twenty for the pass, then handed him a receipt with a piece of tape at the top. John stuck it in his window as they drove through the empty parking lot.

Guess there isn't much sandboarding going on today, he thought.

He was grateful for the ability to park wherever he wanted. They had already missed out on a few different sites. He simply couldn't squeeze the giant vehicle into the packed lots.

When he parked, he turned on the generator, listening to it roll over for a few seconds before finally catching. He took Jake out, walked him into some bushes, ones that looked like they had the least amount of spikes, until the old dog lifted a leg. Jake, long past his adventuring days, had no interest in staying out in the cold, so John walked him back to the motorhome, lifted his back legs up the stairs and patted his bottom as the old hound went back to his bed.

"Who wants to go see the dunes?" John asked, holding the door with a tight grip, keeping the wind from slamming it against the siding.

No one seemed enthused.

All the energy they had on the Zion hikes had disappeared. Erik was on his tablet, watching a cartoon. Stacy was making lunch—tuna sandwiches with carrots and chips. Ellie was looking out the window, out towards the dunes. Maybe she was contemplating going with him.

"El, you want to come?"

She looked back at him, rolled her eyes, then gazed back out the window.

"All right. But this might be the only chance you'll get to see this place," John said with mock disappointment as he slowly shut the door. He laughed at how lame he sounded. Like his own dad not so long ago. Or at least it hadn't seemed that long ago. But he was turning forty on the trip. They would be at the Grand Canyon then. He was already picturing it, his family around him, maybe a birthday cake shared at the park, while they watched the sunset along that vast slit in the earth. He never thought he would turn forty. Now, here it was. And his baby girl, El, was now fifteen and seemed to barely acknowledge his existence anymore.

It started hailing on the walk to the dunes, the small ice pebbles coming down from the sky at a sharp angle.

He stood under the overhang of a man-made platform, looking out onto the dunes that were hemmed in by the surrounding mountains.

The dunes themselves were not as spectacular as he had hoped. But maybe it was just the gloomy weather. The wind had smoothed out any traces of previous visitors. There was something odd, liminal about its emptiness. The hail slowly turned the light orange sand into rippling waves of a stark crystalline white.

An abrupt unnatural movement caught his eye. Something crawled low to the ground on the hill closest to him. He squinted through the hail, trying to make sense of the form he was seeing. It was partially obscured by tufts of grass, but the way the thing moved sent shivers down his spine. He went to the other side of the platform to get a better look, then stepped back, ice lancing through his gut.

It was Ellie.

John called out, but it was carried away by the wind and hail. He ran down, trudging through the sandbanks.

Ellie was on her knees in a low sweep of the dunes. Her back was to him.

A voice, deep down somewhere at the core of him, was telling him to turn around, to get back to his motorhome, to the rest of his family, and drive far, far away.

But that was foolish. This was El.

She was hunched over in her hoodie. Sand trickled into the cuff of her pajama pants.

"El," he called out again, his voice almost a whisper.

El was digging in the sand, slowly, with care, almost reverence. Hail stuck in her hair, in the hood of her sweater.

"Look," she said, turning to him.

John expected to see the face of some monster, black dead doll eyes gazing. But it was just El. His baby girl.

She held a long, jagged rock. Black as night. Obsidian. It was shaped into a blade. Flecked off and razor sharp.

She walked up to him, lifted the blade to his face.

"Look," she said again.

He could see how thin the edges were, how it could flay the skin right off a man without a thought. He saw himself in the blade, gleaming in a hundred warped and smoky reflections. He felt himself falling into that dark pit of black glass.

He tried to scream, but there was only silence within the wind and hail.

John saw the elk again two hours later. It was standing at the edge of a sandstone cave. One of many that pockmarked the side of a mountain. The flames of the elk illuminated the cave, showing the vast subterranean depths.

John watched, entranced, as his motorhome began to slide across the dividing line.

"Dad! Look there's dinosaurs!" Erik called out from the back, breaking John's daydream.

On the billboard, dinosaurs roamed through an ancient landscape. The pockmarked mountain was shown in the background, the holes like black eyes. *One Hundred and Forty Million Years of Natural History!* the sign read.

"It'll be nice for the kids," Stacy said.

John told her that the sandstone caves were not on their list—an exhaustive list of exciting adventures he had painstakingly developed over the previous couple months.

Stacy put her hand on his shoulder, smiled at him. Even El wanted to stop. El who seemed not to want to do anything with her parents for the last year or more. She was peering out the window. In the dim light of the motorhome, she looked just like his little girl, the one that had grown out of wrestling in their living room, grown out of running from him through their hallway, screaming, as he stalked her, draped in a blanket, roaring like some fantastical beast.

He wedged the motorhome into a parking spot that hugged the highway, then got out to check if his rear was sitting in the road, just waiting to be carved off by a passing big rig.

The dinosaur was just some piece of crap fiberglass stegosaurus, hardly bigger than Erik himself. Past the dinosaur, past his family, the carved-out sandstone mountain loomed.

He couldn't see the elk anymore. Not from here. But what else might live within those labyrinthian caves? He couldn't guess. Didn't want to.

The biggest of the caves, the one along the roadside, the one touting the dinosaurs, charged ten dollars a head to enter. Apparently, the cave was once used as a speakeasy. Movie stars, filming westerns, took shelter in the cool underworld to drink and dance. The bar was still there. Head shots of the movie stars hung on the wall, some signed with personal messages. Their tour guide, a hunched and decrepit man in black suspenders, shuffled them through the bar, telling them all this while he waved his hand this way and that.

The old man took them further into the cave, through different informational stands—one on the various ancient pottery found in the cave, another on John Wayne, who was apparently a frequent visitor.

Ellie was standing in front of a glass kiosk far away from the others, as though it wasn't meant to be seen and read.

Obsidian blades sat in a bed of dry straw, gleaming from the magnesium lamp above. The information plate suggested the blades had been used for sacrifices in the cave hundreds of years ago.

"They are beautiful, aren't they?" Ellie said, her finger slowly sliding along the glass.

"Beautiful," he said. Because he couldn't say anything he wanted to say.

The guide took them further into the cave, into the largest section. The light faded. Soon, they were walking through a wall of darkness. In the distance, cave paintings, traced over in dayglo paint, danced across the walls, illuminating the circular chamber in an unreality. Scenes of slaughter, of men holding down another man while a woman sliced him open with a black blade. Rising from her head were the horns of an elk, bathed in flames.

The cave felt warmer. The air humid, choked. As though it was packed full of people.

"This was where the ceremonies took place," the old man said. He looked unnatural in the neon darkness, flared in a corona of foxfire as he recounted the grisly rites, his voice soaring with excitement.

John gaped at the old man, shocked at the horror of all that he was saying. The man's eyes floated in that blackened space, eager, as he continued on, describing to the smallest detail the awful rituals, the flaying of skin, the harvesting of organs.

The fear in his belly began to grow into a trembling panic. The darkness closed in on him. The dancing people in the paintings leered. A breath on his neck made him turn. Ellie was there. Smiling. Teeth and eyes incandescent in the neon blaze.

Leaning against the stegosaurus, still smarting from the glare of the sun, John was smoking a cigarette when Ellie came out from the cave. She told him Stacy and Erik were still in the gift shop.

"Don't tell mom," he said, snuffing out the cigarette.

"Only if you give me one," she said, smirking.

"In your dreams."

He was looking over at the other caves that dotted the hillside.

"You want to check them out?" Ellie said.

They hiked a short trail that hugged the highway, then steadily climbed up the side of a hill along a worn path. The natural stairway was made of a thousand thin layers of red rock and sandstone. He wanted to tell Ellie how beautiful the rocks were, but he felt she'd already listened to enough of his fascination with the geography. So, he kept his mouth shut.

Names were carved in the soft stone. Initials and hearts. A dick and balls. Tits. Even a birthday cake with more candles than he could count.

There was no one on the short hike, no cars on the highway.

A thin layer of fine sand blanketed the floor of the cave, undulating in ripples that reminded him of the dunes. Light shone bright at the entrance, then faded into a darkening gradient of shadows the further they went in. At intervals, where the ancient flow of water had pierced the edges of the mountain, the pockmarked holes poured in webs of sunlight.

He walked to one of the holes. It cast an egg of light on the shadowed sand. He shuffled to the edge, his knees feeling weak from the steep drop. In the distance, there were darkened hills the color of blood. He could see the road below him.

This was where the elk stood. He could feel the warmth of its flames.

"Be careful," his daughter said, putting her hand softly on his shoulder.

"Yes," John said.

He looked out onto the blood-stained hills. Then he felt himself falling, falling.

At their campsite near Bryce, it took John an hour to set up the motorhome. To plug in the electric, the sewage, the water. Block the tires, level it. Set up the dog pen outside. Food and water for Jake. It had become a routine for him, while Stacy prepped for dinner and the kids went off to explore.

He gathered half-burnt firewood from other pits. They sat out in the dark, roasting s'mores, talking. The shadows of the mountains loomed high above, like hunched ogres.

There was no one else at the RV park. There wasn't even an attendant.

Erik was walking through the empty spots, looking for rocks in the gravel.

John sensed something out in the dark was watching his son.

There came the sharp clip of hooves in the shadows.

A scream.

Stacy pointed, and John looked.

Yes, he thought. Yes.

He stood, but it was too late.

John didn't know when he'd awoken. He'd been laying there a long time, listening to the cold wind blowing. At first, he wasn't sure where he was. He still hadn't gotten used to waking up in the cramped dark of the motorhome.

He sat up. There was something trembling, tucked into a tight ball near his feet. It was mewling in the dark.

He reached out then pulled back as fangs flashed.

Jake. The dog was whining now, curling back into a ball, pushing himself further into the corner. What happened? What had he seen?

John stood. The door of the trailer was open. Snow billowed inside the motorhome in gentle gusts. He got up, went to close it.

He knew something was wrong. He checked the overhead sleeper. Erik was asleep, his scrawny chest heaving, his mouth open.

Ellie was gone.

Was he awake when she left? Images of her walking out into the night floated within his mind.

It was a gentle snow, soft, that touched his skin. It dropped out of a sky without clouds, like stars falling. The moon was high above, bloated and staring.

Ellie was standing there, incandescent smile and teeth. Behind her stood the elk, its antlers rising up into the moonlight. It was her crown of fire, of night and stars.

Come back, he wanted to call out for El. Please come back in from the cold, baby. Come on back.

But no words came out.

They never could.

He fell to his knees at the center of that cathedral of stars and snow, wreathed in fire.

He looked up at her, tears in his eyes, thinking of those days playing the monster, crawling around with the blanket covering him, snarling. Those long ago days. He smiled as the cold glinting blade, black as the sky above, bit.

No Exit

Jonathan Reddoch

Wilford was exhausted, but it was early, and he had many miles still to go before he weeps. He never missed a Ballard family reunion, so come *hell* or high water, he would make this one.

He drove past the only exit for Beaver with a chuckle. This was no time for a silly photo-op.

He drove on, passing several exits offering no services.

Small towns, big steeples.

He was getting drowsy. He should have stopped to eat in Beaver. He laughed at an unspoken inappropriate joke.

A sign rose ahead:

"No services."

The I-15 stretched on and on into the frozen horizon.

No church services.

"You are a disappointment."

Granny Henrietta was the family matriarch. This would likely be her last reunion. Uncle Joshua said he didn't think she would last another winter on the farmstead.

Final chance to fill up. Missed the exit.

You will never make it home.

The old woman never forgave him for leaving the flock. For abandoning his covenants. She told the prodigal son his eternal inheritance was forsaken. He had thrown in his lot with harlots and reprobates.

His hell was paved with bad intentions: pearl necklaces and porking.

No service for sinners.

Even if he was shunned this year, the old woman would be receiving her eternal reward sooner or later. And he would be welcomed into the warm bosoms of his cousins.

They would not forsake him. Not forever.

He was teetering. Couldn't keep his eyes awake a second longer.

No soul, no soup, no service.

The bare road stretched on into eternity.

No exit.

Not ever.

The path of his suffering was eternal. Hours, like days, passed.

Finally, there it was. The exit to his grandmother's great and spacious mansion! Did she keep a spare room for him?

But the exit was sealed off.

He was forced to drive on. And on. And on.

There would be no exit in this life.

Or the next.

Route 189

Lehua Parker

The moon was high over Mount Timpanogos on a cloudless night, the kind of night where the stars were diamond chips and the summer air was still and cool. No wonder people moved to Heber. I was fumbling for my Subaru's key when a guy carrying a backpack approached from the house. "Hey!" he called. "Hey!"

I looked up. I didn't know him, but then again, I didn't know a lot of the people at the party. Sylvia collected interesting people for fun. I didn't want to think too hard about what that might say about me.

"Yeah?" I said.

"You Kay... Key..." he slurred.

"Keahi," I said.

"What?"

"Kay-ah-hee." I rolled my eyes, so tired of this. I used to go by my first name, Jacob, but like a lot of island kids, I switched to my Hawaiian middle name when I graduated high school and moved away. There was no turning back now.

At least Tūtū was happy. She never liked Jacob.

He went to snap his fingers but missed. "That's it. Kay-aaah-heeeeee. Hey." He gave me a little wave.

"Hey."

"I'm..." he stifled a burp. "I'm Scott. Sylvia said you could give me a ride back to Provo."

Frick. Somebody always wanting something, I thought. "How'd you get here?"

"Julie. She bailed, like, two hours ago." He grinned. "I gotta get to work by 7 a.m. or I'd just stay here. Sylvia's cool like that. But, like, bills. You know?"

I sighed. "I know. Yeah. Hop in."

"Cool, cool, cool," he said, opening the passenger door and sliding in.

I gave him side-eye. "Just don't barf in my car."

He saluted. "Trying not to, Chief." He pulled two beers from his backpack. "Got us a couple for the road."

I took one. "Thanks." I popped the top. "'Ōkole maluna!'"

"Oh-what?" he laughed.

"Cheers," I said.

"¡Salud!"

We clinked. The icy brew left a trail all the way to my stomach. I rubbed my eyes, then held the bottle to my forehead. *Maybe this is a blessing in disguise,* I thought, stifling a yawn. *Company'll keep me awake all the way down the canyon.*

"Ready?" I said, starting the car.

"Let do this!"

I pulled out of the subdivision and headed west on 12th South toward Provo Canyon.

"Hey, Scott," I said, "I just gotta stop at the Walmart and splash some gas into Subbie. Won't take a minute."

"No prob," he said. "Might go take a whiz." He'd already chugged his beer dry.

While Scott looked for a bathroom, I pumped gas. This late and on the edge of town, the gas station was an island of light in an ocean of darkness. I don't know how the little old lady snuck up on me.

"Ahem," she delicately coughed.

"Holy crap!" I blurted.

"No," she said. "But close."

She was tiny, maybe five feet even. She had long white hair that tumbled down her back in big loose curls. She was wearing a white, long-sleeved, shift-like dress that went to her ankles and what Utahns called flip-flops and I called slippahs on her feet, cheap ones, like from a dollar store. I couldn't see her face clearly, just a hint of a brown nose and age spotted cheeks. *Hispanic,* I thought. *Maybe Native American. Paiute, maybe.*

I laughed nervously. "You scared me."

"Me? A little old native woman scared a big, strapping man like you? Doubt it," she said. She just stood there, staring at me while the numbers on the pump clicked.

"Uh, can I help you?"

"That's not how this works," she said and leaned against my car.

Crazy. Crazy old lady. Worried, I glanced at her and noticed the arthritic twists in her fingers, the swelling in her knuckles. I shook my head, laughing at myself. *Too many slasher movies, brah. She's harmless. Probably just looking for a couple of bucks. I have my emergency twenty in the center console and a Snicker's bar. That I can do.*

I shut off the pump and replaced the hose. Scott bounded up. "No restroom. Store's closed. We'll have to hurry to Provo." He glanced at the woman leaning silently on my Subaru. "What up, Abuelita?"

"Abuelita?" she asked.

"Oh. My bad. Yá át ééh, Masani, right?" Scott shot finger guns at her. "C'mon. I know all the words. I used to date a Navajo girl."

She tipped her head back to look at him better. "Pretty, but dumb," she said. She opened the back door and slid in. "You're taking me to Provo."

"Right on," Scott said, crawling into the front passenger's seat. "Want a beer?"

"No gin?" she said.

"Nah."

"Fine. I'll take the beer."

"Wait a minute," I said.

"What?" asked Scott. "We're already headed that way. Plenty of room."

"But—"

She flicked the bottle top off with her thumb. "Take me to Provo, Grandson," she said.

"See?" said Scott. "Family. I thought you people got that."

"You people?" I asked.

"Yeah." He waved a hand. "You know what I mean."

"No. I don't."

"Oh, Key—"

"Kay," said the little old woman. "It's Kay-ah-hee. Keahi."

"Yeah. That," said Scott. "See? She gets it."

When did I turn into an Uber? I sighed. *No good deed, right?* The sooner I got down the canyon, the sooner this would be over. I started the car and pulled onto U.S. Route 189. Near the airport, I reached for my beer and took a swig.

Scott sat sideways in his seat. "So, I'm—"

"Scott," said the old woman. "I know."

"Oh, good," said Scott. "What should we call you?"

She smiled. "It doesn't matter."

"Masani? Hootse'e?" He grinned. "Yeah, I know a bit of Paiute, too."

She shrugged. "Granny. Abuelita. Aunty. Tūtū. It doesn't matter. I answer to all those and more."

"Cool, cool, cool," said Scott.

We were almost to the last turn off to Charleston when movement in the backseat made me glance in the rearview.

"A dog? How did a dog get in here?" I said.

"She likes car rides," the old woman said.

The little white dog was the size of a chihuahua with a long tail that curved high over her back. As we passed the last streetlight, her eyes flashed red.

A trick of the light, I thought. But I put my beer down.

"Oh, Sweet'ums," Scott gushed. "C'mere, Coco."

"Coco?" I said. "Is Coco your dog?"

"She's her own person," said the woman.

"You tell him, Aunty. Dogs are not owned," said Scott. He clapped his hands. "C'mere, Precious. C'mon!"

I shot Scott a look. "Where did you say you were from?"

"Originally? Ventura. Why?"

I shook my head. "Nothing."

"I love dogs. Growing up in my 'hood, all the abuelitas had a little white dog named Coco or Princess."

"Seriously?"

"Yeah. And they're either angels or demons. And I know this one's an angel, aren't you, Princessa? Come snuggle Uncle Scottie," he said, reaching between the seats.

The dog hissed.

"Her name's Hina," said the woman. "And she's no angel."

Scott turned back in his seat, nonplussed.

"Heber's not Ventura," I said with a shrug.

"I'm not sure that's a dog," Scott muttered. He wiped his face. "I'm, like, baked, dude. I swear that dog hissed like a Komodo dragon."

I caught the woman's eye in the rearview. In the moonlight streaming through the Subaru's sunroof, her hair seemed richer, darker. I blinked. *At the gas station she looked like she was eighty, but she's really closer to forty.* She blew me a kiss and smiled. *Wait. Were her lips always that red?*

"Road," she said pointing forward.

I straighten in my seat and set my hands at ten and two.

"Good choice," she said. "Out here, Route 189's a curvy two-lane road with Deer Creek Reservoir on one side and sheer rocky cliffs on the other. Who knows what could happen?" We passed a couple of memorial crosses, stark in the headlights against the mountainside. "Well, maybe they do." She chuckled.

Like a polar plunge, ice swept across my body, freezing in my armpits and sucking my balls into my throat. Suddenly, I was stone cold sober. I glanced at Scott. He was still feeling no pain, dragon-dog or no.

"So, Abuelita, what's in Provo?" he asked.

Another tight S curve.

"Nothing special. Just an errand I needed to run on my way home."

"Where's that?"

"Far," she said.

"Far? Everything's far from here. What brought you to Heber?" Scott asked.

"Hina and I were visiting family in Wyoming."

"Cody?"

"Yellowstone."

"Yellowstone? Cool, cool, cool. I been there once. Big geysers."

"Lame," she sniffed. "All show, no sizzle." Her voice teasing and coy. And young.

I checked the rearview. The crow's feet at the corners of her eyes were gone. A bare brown shoulder peeked out of the white sarong now tied across her chest. The little white dog grinned on her lap, ears perked. The woman held my eyes in the mirror as she wrapped her long, lush hair into a bun. "Road," she said.

I whipped my eyes forward and swerved back into my lane.

Pele. Pele. Pele. All the stories. It fits. The goddess Pele! In my car! It's never good.

All along the winding road, the moon followed, blazing a trail along the surface of Deer Creek Reservoir, ocean deep and a mile wide all the way to the dam.

"You know what we need? Tunes!" said Scott. He turned on the radio. A whistling warble poured out of the speakers. He fiddled with the dial. Nothing changed. "Ah, man. Just static. Reception sucks in the canyon." He flipped it off. "You got any CDs, man?"

"No," I said.

I caught her eye again. She laid a finger alongside her nose and nodded.

Nose flute, not static.

Oh, shit. It's real.

"Road," she said. "Speed." Her voice as playful as a teen's.

The S curves were faster, tighter now. As much as I wanted to get home, I eased up on the gas a bit.

"No tunes. Bummer. But—" he rummaged in his pack. "That doesn't mean the party's over." He held up a joint. "Do you partake of the herb, mon?"

"No," I said through clenched teeth as Island Beach Park flashed past, the jet skis and boats bobbing in the harbor.

Scott waved the joint high in the air. "Granny? This is some good shit. You're not going to make me do this alone, right?" he said.

"We're never alone," she said.

"Awesome. Sharing is caring." He wiggled in his seat, digging into his pocket. "Damn. I think I left my lighter at Sylvia's."

"I've got a light," she said.

"Perfect," said Scott. "Let's burn this baby."

I felt a warm glow rise over the seatback as the smell of sulfur scorched the hair in my nostrils. A slender young hand with the tip of one finger aflame pushed between the front seats.

Scott turned towards it. "Tha—HOLY MOTHER! YOUR HAND'S ON FIRE!"

"Didn't you want a light?"

"AND WHAT THE HELL HAPPENED TO YOUR FACE?"

I started to hit the brakes.

"Grandson. Deer."

At the last second, I saw it. A doe poised on the right side of the road about to leap. I swerved left. We skidded across the center line.

Scott shrieked, the sound shredding my eardrums like a hot knife through butter.

"Right," she said.

I didn't look. I just reacted, overcorrecting and caroming against the guardrail, scraping paint. In the headlights I saw a flash of dark water below the highway at the same time a truck came over the rise halfway into my lane.

I flinched as our mirrors kissed and shattered.

"FUUUUUUHHHHHH!" shouted Scott as he closed his eyes.

I stood on the brakes, a death grip on the wheel.

The truck continued down the road toward Heber, red taillights dancing down the mountainside, sparkles of broken mirror trailing.

Stopped on the narrow shoulder, pinned against the guardrail and half in the right lane, I shut the engine off. The moon pooled on Subbie's hood, the tick of the cooling engine loud in the darkness. And everywhere, everywhere, the scent of burnt rubber and bare metal.

I rested my head on the steering wheel. "Everyone okay?" I sputtered.

Scott whimpered. "I think I shit myself."

A beautiful young woman leaned between the seats. "You didn't," she said.

"Oh, good," he said.

She patted my shoulder. "Well done, Grandson. Maikaʻi. Thanks for the lift. Hina and I will get out here." She paused. "You know I have many names. But the one I like best—"

"Is Tūtū Pele." I sighed. "Why? Why me? Why us?"

"Mortals," she scoffed. "It's not always about you." She leaned close and kissed my cheek. I felt my skin sizzle. "A little reminder that I do what I do because I want to."

Faster than wisps of smoke from a volcano vent, Pele and Hina melted into the night.

Twenty long years ago. I never saw Scott again after dropping him off along the diagonal in Provo. Some things are too hard to share no matter how much you care. It's the stories we tell. But I know it was real each time I look in the mirror and see Pele's kiss burned upon my cheek.

I remember.

Migration

Cygnus Perry

My winds beat over fields of Autumn grain
I cross roads, unbound by the naked ground
My home, I abandon, left to remain

I traverse tangled rivers in chill rain,
lapping the droplets with my tongue undrowned
My paws trample down fields of Autumn grain

I gallop on gravel, chasing the train
Spittle drips from my lips like a bloodhound
My home, I've forgotten, left to remain

I prowl across mountains now mine to reign
My prey: lost travelers from lands unfound
My scales glide under fields of Autumn grain

I slide through the grape vine and curtain drain,
coiling in myself, around and around
My home, I dream toward, left to remain

I wake in bed, only halfway insane,
I grin with new feeling, new power found
My soul rules over fields of Autumn grain
My home, I've returned, endless domain

Happy Tears

Travis Coleman

My head was throbbing as I woke up. Not the normal hangover type of headache, but more a giant playing a timpani drum. It was hard to think with the throbbing pain in my body. I didn't even realize my eyes were closed for several moments. Only once I opened them did I realize the cause of my pain.

Two Days Ago

For the first time in my life, I felt like I had things aligned. I had a car that would do more than just get me around town, I had money in the bank so I could afford a road trip, and most of all, I had the entire weekend for Thanksgiving off from school. So, I decided I needed to set up a trip home to surprise my family for Thanksgiving. It would be a long drive, but I knew that's what I really wanted to do. I called my parents, hoping that mom or dad would answer and not one of my younger siblings. I felt a wave of relief when Mom answered.

"Hey Mom," I said.

"How are you, Jordan?" she asked. We didn't talk often, but I was always glad to hear her voice on the other end.

"I'm doing pretty good," I said. "So, what time is dinner on Thursday? I was hoping that I could call when everyone was there and wish them a Happy Thanksgiving."

This was the lie, but a little one to help keep my visit a surprise. It was also a chance for her to spread it around to the family back in Washington, while I made my own plans for the drive. Right now, I had most of my stuff I was going to take stacked on the dresser; a couple pairs of underwear, two pairs of pants, a sweatshirt, a couple of t-shirts, and a few pairs of socks. That should be enough to get me there and back, perhaps including a spare shirt in case I spill gravy on one.

"I still wish you could make it down," she said. "You know we could see about getting you a last-minute ticket if you really wanted to come. Your sister is bringing her new boyfriend who she's been dating for a few months. He seems like a nice guy, and I'm sure they'd love to meet you."

"Nah," I said. "You know I really need to focus. I've got a tough load this semester, and if I want to graduate on time, I really need to study. Besides, Alex's family invited me to their place here for food. So I will go there and then see you for Christmas."

"I know Jordan, but I wish that once you're done with school, you'll come back closer. Living in Utah is so far away." I could hear her moving around the kitchen putting away dishes, while in the background I could hear Dad's news going. That was his normal nightly routine. He'd come home, eat dinner, and then make his way into the family room to watch the news. If no one bothered him, he'd be snoring within about twenty minutes. I tried to listen to see if he'd already reached that point. He was still several years from retirement, and we knew that he would live between that chair and the golf course once he was.

"Mom, it'll be okay. I've applied to grad schools all over the west coast. Unless they land me in San Diego for some weird reason, I can almost guarantee that I'll be closer to you."

"I know. You're just the first one of my children who's gone off and away, and I miss having you around the holidays," she said. It wasn't the first Thanksgiving I'd missed, but that didn't seem to make it any easier for her. I heard her sniff and could hear her voice quaver as she spoke. In my head, I could see her heading over to pick up the small box of tissues she kept by the home phone, pulling one free to wipe beneath her eyes, and I almost broke at that moment. The only tears I wanted to worry about were her happy ones, the tears of excitement and surprise she would cry because that's who Mom was. She cried when she was sad, cried when she was proud, and cried when she was happy. Really, any emotion that overwhelmed her would cause her eyes to overflow. I couldn't wait to see her happy tears as I greeted her at home.

We talked late into the night, catching up on the family news. While we talked, I spent my time packing my bag and getting ready to go. I didn't say goodnight until almost eleven o'clock when Mom insisted she had to get Dad up and move him to bed. I fell asleep with the phone on my chest.

...Happy Tears...

The thought slowly drifted through my head. It had been something of a mantra the entire drive up here. That was what I was excited about. That was what I had kept telling myself but the throbbing in my head pushed the thought from my brain. I was confused at what I was seeing as I tried to look around. In front of me was a deflated balloon, and the whole area smelled of burnt rubber. My head was forced down, meanwhile my ear drums were pulsating like I'd been doing too many push-ups without breathing.

The edges of my vision started to darken, and I felt a moment of vertigo as I tried to orient myself. I reached to my waist and tried to find the seat belt. That was part of the pain across my chest, as it was holding me in like a rag doll. It took several seconds, each one punctuated with the throb of pain in my head. My temples felt like I'd be sprouting horns at any moment, and I wanted to clutch my head, but I kept my focus long enough for my fingers to find the release, and with a click the seat belt released me.

I half fell, half slid to the roof of the car. I say 'half fell' because there wasn't anywhere to really go now that the airbag wasn't in my face. The wheel caught my legs for a moment, and then I managed to army crawl my way past the seat to lay flat. I lay on the roof of the car, stretched out as much as I could while I took inventory of where I was and what was happening. My eyes wanted to close, but I fought to keep them open. I needed to take stock of my situation.

I was lying on the ceiling of a car which meant gravity was pulling me that way. The car ceiling was not nearly as tall as I remembered, so the car top had been crushed down. As I breathed, the car breathed with me, and the cold seeped in around me. I was missing windows.

Where was I?

Yesterday

The grocery store was mayhem as people scampered around each other looking for the items they'd forgotten on their list. Everything had to be perfect for Thanksgiving, so the day before and the day after obviously had to be a war zone at the stores. I was so glad that I only needed to hit the candy aisle, the cookie aisle, and grab a couple of energy drinks.

I had slept in this morning until about noon, and I knew that I would need about ten hours to get from Cache Valley to the Tri-cities where my family lived. As long as I set out by ten tonight, I should be there in time for breakfast. That even accounted for gas stops, and if I needed a break from driving on the way there.

In my basket I already had dry roasted peanuts and beef jerky for protein. I looked at the crackers on the shelf in front of me, trying to decide between Wheat Thins, Cheez-its, and Club crackers. The box of club crackers would be better because I liked their buttery flavor more than the saltiness of the other two. The drink aisle was almost abandoned compared to the rest of the store which made grabbing the energy drinks and the water a breeze. When I reached the checkout counter, I waited for my turn. Despite my resolve that I had my snacks, a couple of packages of peanut butter M&M's found their way into my cart. After all, I might want something sweet to provide more variety in my snacks. Now I was ready to go on the road trip. I took my receipt and headed out to my car, an older Toyota Corolla that I'd bought last year after doing summer sales in Tennessee. It wasn't much, but it got me around, had new tires that I'd purchased, and ran well. Really, what more could a guy just starting out ask for?

I placed the snacks in the passenger seat and buckled myself in. It was still noon, so I had time to go and play some video games, or maybe study for a bit before I left. I mean, I even had time for a nap. I knew this would probably be the most important preparation if I was going to be driving all night.

A few minutes passed as the blood left my temples and redistributed itself back through my body. As it did, some of the pain subsided, and I was able to take stock of my situation. I looked around and could only see a bit of light coming from the dashboard. Most of the warning lights were red, but it was barely enough to see by.

Where was I? I found myself asking as I tried to look around and find my cell phone. That would have GPS, the ability to call emergency services. I moved around the cab along the ceiling, the whole area littered with the various wrappers I had in the cab. I saw two empty cans from the energy drinks I'd had. There was the box of crackers which I believed still had some in there. Then there was the half-empty one liter bottle of water I'd grabbed at my last stop. I couldn't seem to find the phone though. I started checking the console above me, the panic of my situation starting to make my heartbeat increase. With each pulse, I could feel not only my anxiety raise, but also my light-headed-ness increased. As the center console opened, several items fell out—a phone charger, a pair of headphones, a set of nail clippers, and my wallet. I felt tears forming in my eyes as the panic set in fully. The heartbeat increased as I slowly lost consciousness.

Several Hours Earlier

I was making my way past Twin Falls when I first noticed the storm. It started as a bit of rain at first, but after a few minutes, I started to see the shape of snowflakes on the windshield. I looked at the time on my radio and saw that it was just after eleven-thirty. The traffic wasn't bad at this hour, but there was way more than I would expect due to the holiday. Once the rain changed to snow, the traffic became something else entirely. The rain had started off light, but within twenty minutes, the snow was accumulating along the side of the roads, and the cars around me were leaving marks of the path most traveled. Between the tires, the snow looked brown and slushy. As I changed lanes, I could feel the slush pulling against the tires.

I didn't feel like I wanted to pass, but the traffic which had been humming along at eighty-five now had fallen to fifty-five, and I had a schedule to keep. I knew what I needed to do, and I'd driven on snowy roads before. I had been going to school in Utah for four years after all, and where I grew up in Washington had their fair share of bad winters. They both had hills, mountains, and snow, so I knew I would be okay. It made me wonder why everyone here in Idaho didn't know how to drive in the snow.

I reached over and turned up the radio, blasting the music, and sped along as quickly as I could. I knew it was going to be a long night, and so I tried to sing along with the playlist I'd made earlier. It was only a bit longer until I would be home, this drive would be over, and I'd be able to see everyone around me cry of joy.

...Happy Tears...

I couldn't tell how long had passed before I woke up because there were no longer any lights from the dashboard. What woke me up was a sound from outside the car, the sound of metal straining and beginning to bend. I looked around and tried to see what was happening, but before I could, the seats in the car dropped about half a foot, the space between the headrests and the seats disappearing in a moment. In that same moment, my senses lit up in pain. My left leg had been beneath the seat back when it dropped. Now that it had collapsed, my left leg was pinned mid-shin. I began to scream and started kicking at the seat back, hoping that I could get it to give way. I felt the weight pressing down on my shin, and I worried that my leg would snap in half. Again, my heartbeat increased, but this time I could feel a warm stickiness spreading on my temple. I ignored it as best I could as I kept kicking, but the seat didn't want to give. I paused, gasping for air, and in the moment tried to clear my mind.

I looked at the situation and tried to figure out what I would do. My brain chose this moment to interject the thought that this was what the seats were designed for. They were designed to hold up to crashes and not bend or fold under the weight. I shook my head, wondering how that was supposed to help things, but instead I found myself laughing. Of course, the thing keeping me stuck in the car, unable to open doors, unable to squeeze out under the gap, was good engineering. I hoped some guy in his office was happy with his design choices, I thought as I continued to laugh.

It took me a few moments before I got a hold of my emotions and noticed that I was feeling clammy. The exertion must have really taken it out of me. I unzipped my hoodie and ripped it off, throwing it across the car, and began to kick the car seat again and again. I didn't need much. I needed the seat to give a bit and then I could get my leg out. I continued kicking until the world began to swim again, and then my vision went dark.

Two Hours Earlier

I watched the flashing lights of the plow trucks as they passed me. I wanted to pull forward, but all the spots were occupied at the front of the store. I needed to get out and stretch my legs for a minute. Needed to get my fingers off the wheel of the car because I was beginning to fear that I wouldn't be able to unclench them after the last five hours of driving. It was four a.m., and I needed an energy drink and a liter of water. A part of me felt I should grab something else, but I couldn't think of what.

I pulled on my hoodie and walked across the lot between the pumps and the store. I could see most of the cars had people in them. Most had engines running and people trying to sleep. That was good. The fewer people on the road, the less likely they were going to do something stupid or end up in a wreck. Even with the bad weather and slower speeds, I needed like four or five more hours, and I'd end at home. I should be there by nine or ten a.m., in time to help put the turkey in the oven for dinner.

The store was full, people blocking the aisles. I had to ask several times for people to move so I could get to the cooler. Despite the whole place being super busy at four a.m., no one was waiting to check out. Less wait, more speed. I'd be back on the road and home even faster.

As I stepped back out into the cold, I could see the snow had accumulated almost half an inch on the ground. The hood of my car, which stuck out from under the edge of the covered pumps, already looked like it needed to be brushed off. Oh well, it'll blow off once I get going again. A few more hours, and I'll be home.

Why had it gotten so cold? I asked myself as I came to. I was shivering, and I couldn't feel my left foot. I tried to take in my surroundings, but there was no light at this point. All around me was darkness. I felt around for my hoodie or my phone or really anything that could give me light or warmth. My hands fumbled through some wrappers, the bottle of peanuts, and then found the fabric of the hoodie. I pulled it over and tried to find the right way to put it on. My joints were stiff, and my fingers struggled to find the holes that I put my arms in.

"I was just wearing you!" I screamed into the darkness, almost as though that would help me find where the hole was. I shook it again and then tried to put it on, and this time my arm slipped through the sleeve. I also realized I was starving. I'd only had snacks all last night because I was planning on having a big dinner today. I rustled through the wrappers again and this time found the box of club crackers. It wasn't much, but I needed it to keep going. I needed to wait longer. Someone would find the car. Someone would come for help. They had to come for help.

An Hour Before

I'd looked at every truck stop, every rest area, and almost every one was closed. Cars had lined the roads into and out of each rest area. The truck stops were all packed with semis. Almost no one was out on the road, so I kept cruising. It had been like this through Baker City and into La Grande, so I'd continued on into the mountains above La Grande. Maybe when I got to the other side in Pendleton, or at the turn off to the Tri-Cities area, there would be a place to stop. At that point, I could catch my breath. I had to make it through.

I looked at my clock and saw it was about six a.m. I still had time. I could still make it by nine or ten if I held on. The hills were a tough climb, but I knew I could do it. I had put on new all-season tires this summer, and so I knew it would be a quick up and over.

I watched the signs as I went up the hill. Kamela, Meacham, and then into the Umatilla Reservation. The roads were white but pass-able; the tracks of the previous vehicles that went in front of me were faint at best. It was all going to be fine until I reached the summit. There, the weather took a turn for the worse, and I found myself blanketed in a sheet of white. The edges of the roads faded to nothing, and I turned my wipers up to high hoping it would compensate. I even found myself sitting forward off the back of my seat, hoping that the little distance I gained between myself and the windshield would give me some kind of sign of what was happening.

Was there a car in front of me? I didn't know. Was someone coming up behind me to try to pass? I had no idea. The only thing that existed was my hood and the six inches of light coming from my headlights before the snowflakes ate up the rest of it.

I tried to cast my mind back into my driver's education training. Was I supposed to get over to the side of the road? If I did and someone came up behind me, would they be able to see me in time? I really didn't know what to do. My fingers began to feel the strain as I squeezed the wheel. At the corners of my eyes, I felt tears forming. I didn't want to cry. I couldn't cry, though, because I couldn't risk losing any more of my vision. I glanced at my rear-view mirror and saw nothing but black. No headlights. No road reflectors. It was just black.

As I looked in front of me at the road, I caught a glimpse of a green sign to my right telling me that I was in the right location. Well, telling me I was on the road. The lettering shined in the light, and I caught what it said in the momentary flash.

Deadman's Pass 1 Mile.

I knew where I was now and knew that I was near the top of the pass. That was good, because it told me that once I passed that exit—if I could see the exit—I would be on the way down the hill and should drop below the storm. While I hadn't been to church much since I'd moved away from my parents, I found myself praying at that moment.

I looked at my speedometer and saw that I was still cruising along at thirty. I wasn't sure if that was too fast or too slow. I stared at it for a moment, trying to decide if I should slow down or not. As I looked back up, one of my questions was answered. Yes, there were cars in front of me.

The red lights of the back of a semi glowed in front of me. I felt adrenaline surge and couldn't help but smash both feet down, trying to stop myself. My feet didn't cooperate the way I wanted them to, while my hands did their own thing in panic. I swerved to the left, my left foot hitting the brake, while my right foot also tried to hit the brake. The car began to spin, sliding down the hill with continuing momentum. My feet continued their stomping, and for whatever reason, the engine sounded like it was over revving. I turned out of the curve, and the car continued to spin. For a moment, I could see the semi cab's driver door, and then it was gone again, and the spin intensified. I remembered in a moment of lucidity that it wasn't turning away from the curve but *into* the curve that would get me out of it. I spun the wheel desperately, my feet continuing their dance on the pedals. I felt the car coming back under my control, and I took a deep breath. That was when the car hit the beginning of the guardrail.

In that moment, I felt my mind slow as everything took on a bit of weightlessness. The car made a grinding noise beneath my feet, and then it was gone. Instead, gravity started to reorient around the car. I knew what this meant, that I was about to roll over. I reached down into the center console and grabbed my phone. I'd need it to call for help once this stopped. Then I could get—

The impact of the car into a tree on the driver's side deployed the front airbags. At that moment, I felt my hands fly out and glass shatter. The safety glass on the windshield was fine, but the side windows were missing. This was followed by another spin and another roll. I felt my head hammer against the back of the seat and then against the frame on the driver's side as the rolls continued. As the car jarred against another obstruction, I hit my head again, and that was the last thing that I remembered.

The water is frozen. It has been for I don't know how long. I've lost track of the number of times I've passed out or gone back to sleep. My fingers are feeling like they're buzzing, and I can't feel anything below the shin on my left leg save a throb from where it's pinned. Why is it so cold? Why did this all happen?

"It's going to be okay," I hear from in front of me. There lying next to me in the car is my mom. She's got her apron on, and I can feel the warmth radiating from her. "You did your best, son. Come here."

She beckons me in for a hug, and now it's my turn to smile at her touch. As she wraps her arms around me, the cold retreats, and I find myself starting to cry. I look at her face and see she is crying too. The warmth spreads through me, and I feel like it's all going to be okay. As I close my eyes one last time, I can feel tears running down my cheeks. My last thought as I'm rocked in my mother's hug is about my happy tears.

Inherited

Lawrence Dagstine

Heaven knows, you never meant any of this to happen. But of course, people will not accept that as an excuse if they ever learn the truth about you.

There has always been a touch of ruthlessness in your nature. People used to say you were the sort of person who wouldn't harm a fly.

Boy, were they wrong.

And how did they not suspect that your dormant trait of ruthlessness could grow under the right conditions?

"Mother," you say, "do you really think I could hurt anybody?"

Mom studies you and seems to wince. "That depends on your definition of hurt. But yes, I could see you harming somebody under the likeliest of circumstances," she says, sitting across the way from you at the dinner table. "Perhaps the gossip among the people of this place will die away in time. Not everybody knows, which is a good thing for *you.*"

You stare over at her, fork in midair, a boy's earlobe oozing blood and scabby puss at the end of it. You are being called on to perform in public for the fifth time other than in truck-stop restaurants, where you're sometimes appointed to negotiate for extra packets of ketchup and sugar. You have a flair for these dramatics, monster that you are, having played the role first as a chubby toddler to whom nothing could be denied. Then, as you had grown older, becoming thin, almost frail, you had learned that plaintive eyes and a pouting mouth could be as profitable as a cherubic face. Perhaps the waitresses, thin and plaintive themselves, saw the cannibalistic determination in your eyes and thought to themselves, what's a dollar's worth of ketchup if it helps this kid not eat people?

But now you hesitate, wondering what the unpracticed answer to all this could possibly be. "I like eating," you say finally. "I like animal flesh too, because it smells good and tastes good."

It always tastes good, doesn't it?

The first thing you notice, the very first thing that shows itself in the fall glare that makes everything look nice and tasty, is the victim outside your window, heading to town. You expect something less methodical—you *always* do—perhaps a mercy killing or hankering down for a small bite before throwing slabs of meat into Mom's cauldron. You shudder as you remember taking a whiff of that last dismembered arm, your insides cold and clammy, and your stomach growling.

"Let's have some meat," Mom said, and she drew the children into the dining room with her. "They can have a taste, can't they?" she asked you. You heard gaiety in her voice, and she smiled at all your brothers and sisters while slicing fatty tenderloins of your last catch into her finest bowls. She handed the first bowl to you, the provider.

You cupped both hands under the bowl and pushed it up to your mouth. Mom had added the most amazing broth to give it flavor.

You usually eat from beneath your house, where you sleep beneath an accumulation of blankets. The oven in the kitchen helps keep part of the house warm, and your family has closed off other rooms so that you live solitary in the last bedroom and scamper up the chilly porch to the kitchen and bath. After all, you're dangerous. Mom doesn't want you near your siblings at certain hours.

Now you stand on your tippy toes and stare out the boxed window. There has never been an autumn like this one. The dogwoods that edge the pines near your next victim's house turn red as blood. The days are still as the sun moves farther away into a haze of changing seasons. Finally, the wind comes, turning the pines into giant brooms that brush endlessly across the sky. Utah's Red Rock wilderness calls to you. The steep cliffs and sandstone that edges the trees call to you. It calls to your voracious appetite, and the gastric juices inside your belly which stir once more.

Your family is keeping you as safe as they can, when what they really want is for you to carry out the necessary grocery shopping that *they* can't. So, for now, they have you locked in a blue-wallpapered room that has green and white furniture and a comforter on the floor with ruffles at the sides. You see that room as disappointing, but it's the best Mom can do. The windows seem too high for escape, but occasionally you manage. You always do. There is no place more secret than this. It's your personal retreat. And where it doesn't offer comfort, it makes up for it with a picturesque view of the National Forest and Salt Flats.

You softly walk up the wide steps into the main hall dimly lighted with frosty sconces, past the room where your father died, past the useless nursery, into the hidden space where, amid the clutter of your child life, photographs, and heavy scrolled furniture, a part of you *is* truly human.

The bed is high with a faint smell of bath powder in it. The smell itself is intoxicating, but soon you turn around and discover your father. The scent quickly becomes foul with the odor of death.

Dad wanted to snatch life away as you have, and yet old worries bogged him down to where he's now a musty corpse in a ripped armchair. Funerals are expensive. And revealing. The future seemed to move tediously, just outside his grasp. You used to hear him before he was up, already fixing sandwiches for the kids, coaxing Mom against dawdling, yelling sometimes when his patience wore thin.

But here he is, stationary, in a very permanent sort of way, and *he* the worse for it. You never knew what had gotten into him, only that you had inherited it, taking your appetite to the next level, although every time you went out hunting for the family, he liked you better. Sitting evenings in his parlor, he felt alive, fearless. Because he had *you*. You think you don't care, but nothing could be further from the truth.

"Mom, I'm leaving now," you say.

"Be careful," she calls out, doing her needlework behind a closed door.

"Make sure the kids are locked up," you add. "I'm in the next hall. I'm about to pass through."

"We're having vegetables tonight, too," Mom says. "Take whatever or whomever you bring home straight to the kitchen, dear, and I'll get the children washed up."

You hold a cold sack against your sweater. Freshness is important in this ritual, refrigeration *essential*. The hallway seems shorter than before, not a shadowy passageway but a lived-in place with just enough light to illuminate both the way and the framed photographs that speak of your ancestors' past.

You exit the house, and the sky splits open. Lightning, a blazing butcher knife among the windblown black clouds, cuts jagged slices in the stirred-up heavens, just like you cut slices out of your prey. Rain pours from the slits as you race for shelter.

The interior of the barn is pitch-black, as dark and cool as the inside of a car at night when you are heading for the next feeding station. You used to sleep best with the whirring of an engine, the rippling highway that used to rock you when you were a baby, carrying you wherever your parents wanted to go next. The authorities were always on your tail, easing up behind you like a bandit taking his victim by surprise.

You ignore the chilling rain and thunder that shake the wooden structure. This evening, the weather has its own hunger. The rain brings with it a torrent of its own feelings, and squatting against the barn's worn side, you see how much you despise doing this. No point in spitting out second thoughts that will only ferment like vinegar on the brain. You have a family to feed. You focus back on your objective, grab your moped, and drive out.

When you enter the ice cream parlor with its old-fashioned soda counter, you see the victim because you are looking at everything. For now, you are feeding on your surroundings. Josh, the Mormon boy who lives just a few houses down, doesn't notice you until you start tugging at his arm and nodding toward the counter. "Mind if I sit?" you whisper. Charm, hidden in years of indecision and captivity, edges your soft voice.

"Please do," he mutters indifferently, although he is pleased that the first person he sees is somebody he recognizes.

You plop down next to him.

The stool had once been a spinner, but now it leans precariously on its pedestal. You put your arms on the counter to keep from slipping off. The boy nods to the server and orders a root beer.

"Orange," you say. You stare at him openly, not bothering with sidelong glances, while he studies the blood and grit under your fingernails.

"I'll have an orange cream, too," he says now. He pushes the watery root beer away as though it didn't belong to him.

"Josh. Josh Hamilton, right?" you ask. "Whatcha know, buddy?"

"Aw, nothing much." He finds himself forced to look straight at you and then past you at the highway patrolman sitting in the corner booth. Nervous, he thumps the lever on the straw dispenser heavily so that two drop out.

"I'm your neighbor up the trail," you say.

"I know who you are. You live in that weird-angled cellar, don't you?"

You flash him a smile. "Yes. I saw you outside my window. This past weekend you helped my mom paint the porch, and now I've come to town to repay you in kind."

The boy suddenly thinks the conversation is beyond his grasp. He looks around you at the patrolman again. "What do you know?" he says glumly. "Oh. Where are my manners? Can I get you something to eat?"

"No, thank you." You dismiss the offer and eye your next mark from head to toe. You're suddenly thinking about cooking this five-foot-eight kid on a spit and concocting your own mayonnaise and barbecue sauce recipes in your head. "I'm about to eat."

Despite your predatorial behavior and the minimal exercise you get, you managed to stay thin through puberty. Sure, your mother forces you to scrub your face with medicated soap and shave occasionally, so you look proper. Appearances are deceiving but also everything. You even inherited your father's razor. On this occasion, you consent to a pair of candy-striped jeans and a purple knit shirt. White, crepe-soled shoes round out the wide-bottomed outfit.

"Not much going on," the boy says. "There's never really much going on in this town."

"I'm going to take a walk in the woods, just mess around some," you go on happily. You sip your soda daintily. "I was wondering if you'd like to come with me."

The boy puffs up. "Where in the woods exactly?" he asks suspiciously.

"The stream," you say. "Maybe toss some rocks."

"How are we supposed to get there?"

"Drive. I have a ride." You nod toward the window.

The boy drops his jaw. "Whoa. You've got a moped?" He bounces on the rickety stool, and you grab his arm to keep him from falling off.

"It's Mama's," you admit. "But I've got it for today. So long as I bring something back to eat for the family. I can give you a ride home afterward." You are grinning uncontrollably.

"Where you going to park though?" he asks. "The stream is down a wide slope, and the incline gets deeper the further you go into it."

"Then we can just ride around and look at things," you say.

"Look at what?" The boy becomes dumber by the minute. Girls generally ignore him so completely that he is totally unprepared for conversation with someone like yourself.

"At anything and everything!" Eventually you are exasperated and turn to him. "Can we just go for a ride?"

He looks over your shoulder at the patrolman once more. "I guess so," he says slowly. He wants to ride around with you, but the idea frightens him a little.

"Please, Josh." You pat his arm convincingly.

You chat some more. In the end, your strong-mindedness overrides his judgment. It comes so easy to you, this intimacy with which you have to take such tremendous care. With *all* your prey.

"You finished with that, young man?" the counter girl finally asks him, nodding at the orange soda which has maybe a quarter left to it and lost most of its fizz. She wants to clean up.

The boy slides his glass over. "I'm done."

He pays for both of you, as any young gentleman would, and you both exit the parlor.

The rain ceases. You find yourself listening intently to the boy as he rides in back of you on the moped, holding onto your waist for dear life. He has loosened up, which should make things easier for you.

Long before you reach the place where you know the other skeletons lie, bodies you picked clean weeks earlier, you begin to think about a bag that hangs from a single tree branch. It's similar to the one which is cold to the touch and tied to your belt loop. The moon, still in infancy, hasn't risen above the trees yet, and the area of the stream lays in the cold blue shadow of the forest. Fate has been kind, in a way. The autumn rains have covered the bodies. Almost. Fighting back tears, you park the moped at the top of the clearing and now force yourself toward the pine with its hanging bag. You lean on it like a starved animal. Shaking it. Shaking it. Shaking it some more.

"Hey, wait up!" the boy hollers, trying to catch his breath. "What're you doing?"

An unusual darkness spills above the sky above the stream, bringing a bitter and sudden chill to the air. You try your best to make the boy comfortable, but he has very little time left on this earth. You suddenly remember your father's nighttime stories. You remember the modern horror tales of men being eaten by other men in rural country. You dare not repeat your father's stories to strangers, because no one would believe such chatter without binges of scared men running around turning all shades of red and begging for mercy on their knees afterward. You didn't even talk about the other four boys, close in age—the ones who got just as lost to your appetite and who are long dead.

"It's all part of the ritual," you finally say.

"Huh?" The boy is confused.

The bag falls two feet away from you. You lean over and pick it up.

"Here," you say, and toss the bag over to the boy's feet.

"What's this?" he asks.

"Put it on," you say. "Over your head."

"Why?"

"Trust me. It's not good. The pain of feeling it is bad enough. The pain of seeing it is far worse. And I have to get home to my family. My brothers and sisters are hungry. *I'm* hungry."

The chunks of flesh you'd taken from the dead boy's skeleton provided what felt like a sumptuous feast. You build a small fire by the edge of the stream, sit Indian style in front of it, and start cooking. You roast what was once a child's eyeball at the end of a gnarled branch, only two inches away from the hot flames. You throw sticks into the fire as you snack, your storage bag behind you filled to capacity. Mom will be happy. More than enough leftovers, and she can finally fill the freezer back up.

You keep the flames leaping high, with a huge bed of coals beneath giving out heat. Funny, you think, how little it takes to be happy when you have something to eat. When on the road you'd discovered how unhappy you could be with almost nothing, you'd made a profound decision. You said, "One day I'm going to be just like my daddy. One day I'm going to provide for my family."

By the end of the night, you intend to divest yourself of the fleshy holdings that give you wealth but never a moment of unhappiness. The decision fills you with more joy than you could ever think possible. After all, you're doing what's right... right?

To come from a family that possesses nothing but the full abundance of the heart to then inherit a full stomach; even now the very idea moves you to tears.

You wipe your eyes and see among the trees, glowing with the reflection of the fire, the spirit of your father. He'd triggered the dormant trait of ruthlessness which you possess now, his fear of it, and had come to an understanding. It happened right after you were born, your mother coddling a half-starved baby in back of a station wagon. Dad seemed ill at ease, painfully incapable of anything but embarrassment. He couldn't even afford formula. The other children, with their stares and scrawny bodies, looked like mouth-moving statues. Only you seemed to have the spark.

You had been born a squalling knot of tight, unexplainable longings that screamed, "I will inherit a trait" to a world that seemed to ignore you and your family, that gave you no safety but the battered shell of an automobile and an armrest on which to pound your silent anger. Now you have a place to draw your longings out slowly, carefully, one victim at a time, and keep everybody from starving.

Not Yet For You

G.D. Watry

My abuelo met La Llorona on a riverbank when he was seven years old. He tells me this on his deathbed, muttering over heart monitor blips that mesh with the heater's static and clunky hymn.

"I washed my family's clothes in the murky water," he says, his milky gaze set beyond the desert shack's smudged window. "I sung lullabies with the rustling reeds, our murmurs accompanied by the babbling river. And there she stood, clad in an ivory dress, her veil billowing beneath a crown of thorns."

He wheezes these words, these ramblings of a dying man, of an oxygen-starved brain.

I sit at the foot of his bed, my hand resting on a blanketed shin, waiting for the inevitable, for the sound of the flatline. I rode from the golden hills of the Pacific Coast to the red, iron-rich clay just to be with my abuelo, the last of my kin. I viewed my life in the west as an escape from this life, from my family, from the off-the-grid living my abuelo raised me with. But the past always has a way of finding you.

Outside, sunset sucks light from the parched, cracked earth; dust whorls flitter over the mesa, ascending upwards into the nightfall, particulate matter transformed into starbursts.

"She slipped secrets in the wind with death's dried tongue," he says. "Terrible visions of unrealized inevitabilities. Blood seeped from my family's festering flesh."

My abuelo's breath hitches in his chest. His tobacco-stained mustache twitches at the gloaming's onset.

Coyotes yelp at a rising, orange slice moon buoyant in an inky molasses. Inside the shack, flames pirouette catastrophic in a limestone hearth, casting a glow against the encroaching darkness.

"'These things will pass for all my children,' La Llorona said to me. 'But not yet for you.'"

My abuelo weeps to his God, his hushed mewls dampened by a mesmeric dreamscape. Consciousness sputters black, and I dream the scene by the river, my view omniscient in this transmitted remembrance.

My abuelo's just a boy. He wades into the river, the water rising up to his waist, heading for La Llorona's open embrace. Skeletal arms ensnare him; she hugs him to her breasts. And with a swift motion, she dunks him in the river and holds him there. My abuelo struggles against her weight, his limbs flailing. She holds with all her might until her arms feel flaccid and ache with numbness. She wrangles and twists, until the snap of breaking bones prickles my brain. Doused in water up to her tattered blouse, she holds until the thrashes hiccup and quell, the water oscillating in the aftermath. And then she lets go.

Now, a crimson caul marbles the moon's pocked surface. A death rattle pierces the amniotic atmosphere.

Awakened, I see her hovering above my abuelo's bed. Her cactus maw spreads wide, splitting his dry lips. My abuelo's eyes shine black oblivion in the blood moonlight.

"These things will pass for all my children," La Llorona says, turning, allowing death's gaze to glimpse me. "But not yet for you."

About Those Hostels the Cute Guy You met at the Underground Vampire Club in Salt Lake City Told You to Try

Juleigh Howard-Hobson

...some words of advice, take them or leave them:
don't talk to anyone when you arrive,
no matter what they ask. Do not become

drawn into conversation about your
family and friends, or lack thereof. There is
no good reason for them to wonder where
you're headed next or how long you plan to
stay in Utah. They're not making small talk.
They don't make small talk. They mesmerize through

conversation to find out exactly
how much trouble drinking your blood will be.

The Road to Ciel

Johnny Worthen

It was a rough road, neglected for the interstate that ran parallel some fifty or sixty miles to the north. He'd chosen it for the lack of traffic but regretted his choice now as he held his thumb out to the empty highway while the daylight faded, darkness crept up, and not a car had driven by in an hour.

The old Honda was in a ditch three miles back. He meant to leave it somewhere along this road, but the crash was unexpected. It was out of sight until someone took that road or some low plane got curious about the sun-faded, baby-blue Accord, ass up in the middle of nowhere. Maybe days. Maybe weeks. Maybe never. He still wasn't sure what he'd hit to career him off the blacktop — animal or one of the craters that passed for a pothole on this neglected stretch of asphalt. Was he still on reservation land? That might explain the road conditions and the lack of traffic. He'd never been to this side of this rez, so it might be.

As he looked around, he saw a new glow on the distant horizon—headlights at magic hour giving him hope that he wouldn't have to walk all the way back to civilization.

Tyson combed his finger though his hair to freshen up before he thought to check his hands. Looking now, he saw they were clean enough. His fingernails would need some attention, but it wasn't obvious now since it was getting dark. He felt his pockets, zipped his jacket, put on his best smile, and saluted the coming vehicle with the timeless call of the hitchhiker, a thumbs up. Positive and friendly. It was an ancient symbol that went back to the Romans. The emperor with his judging thumb would choose life or death for a vanquished gladiator. Everyone knows that, but what Tyson knows, and what few others ever learn, is that thumbs up was not life but death. 'Send the bastard to God,' was the meaning. How it got turned around, he didn't know. He smiled remembering all this and seeing his thumb silhouetted in the light of the approaching car.

If he had, Tyson was prepared to walk. He'd done plenty of walking. His tasks necessitated distant places — seldom visited, lonely places. Quiet places. Such places were magical to him for the feeling of completion they brought, always and deeply the feeling of power. Many times, too many times to recall, he'd had to walk many miles from those lonely silent places. Getting cars stuck in places no modern person was ever meant to be was practically his signature. He wondered if anyone had put that together yet. Started a list. Probably not. No one was even looking.

The car approached, and Tyson twisted his face into some mixture of hope, sincerity, and harmlessness.

The car passed him at speed but then — glory be — the pale road leading on flared crimson red as the car braked and stopped.

Tyson ran the few steps to its side. Knowing the etiquette, he bent down and looked in the window before trying the door handle.

"Can I bum a ride from you a ways?" he asked the driver.

The driver was a white man. Good and bad. Tyson being white himself might suggest camaraderie, but the Indians were usually more accommodating for rides by and large.

"I'm going a ways," said the driver. "Climb in. I'll take you."

"Thanks, Mister."

The car was a classic gold Lincoln Continental Mark V. This particular one was from 1978. He knew that because there was a diamond set in the oval rear windows to celebrate the diamond jubilee of the Ford company. He knew this because he was born that year and had a fondness for special things from then. At the time the car was released, it was the most expensive vehicle Ford had ever sold. Today, it was a dinosaur, an impractical gas-guzzling, massive two-door behemoth with an acre of hood and an eight-track player built into the dashboard.

"Original paint?" Tyson said as he joined the driver in the front bench seat.

"You know it," said the driver. In the dim illumination before he closed his door, Tyson took in the man behind the wheel. Like the car, he was an anachronism. Short sleeved button-down shirt, paisley patterned, pants of some kind. Blue, but not jeans. Matching his belt buckle, he wore a big silver watch that probably needed winding. The shirt was unbuttoned one too many for some people, but it showed a thin gold chain around the man's neck, some kind of charm at the end. But it was his face that really struck Tyson. The man had dark eyes and a heavy mustache with long sideburns. The two did not meet, but both were thick and dark, the one rounding the mouth, the other dropping down to his jawline. His hair was done forward. If the man was wearing square sunglasses and lost the mustache, he could be an Elvis impersonator. As is, he sort of looked like a hard-ass Burt Reynolds.

Tyson stuck out his hand. "Jeff Rogers," he said as introduction.

The man raised an eyebrow at that but took the offered hand and returned a solid handshake. "People call me Berith," he said.

"Pleased to meet you."

The big V8 engine brought the heavy car to cruising speed in no time—the road was much better here—and the two rode in amicable silence. It was important when hitchhiking to talk only as much as the driver wanted conversation. No quicker way to be dropped off early than to be a chatterbox or a taciturn weirdo.

The western horizon had only the faintest hints of last daylight, and to the east, the stars were already bright and plentiful even for the shining moon sharing its sky. A warm desert highway far from the light pollution of cities was a joy to itself. Another one of those lonely places he loved so well.

He glanced at his companion, Berith, and sized him up for special treatment. There was much to recommend it to Tyson. The car being first and foremost on the list. He'd always wanted a car like this. No, not like this. He'd always wanted *this* car. And there was this night, this brilliantly beautiful, lonely night that would be a delight to work in. He'd just finished his last task and usually gave himself a few days or weeks to relish it before starting again, but this might just be too good to pass up. He put his hand in his pocket to feel his knife, finding it still a little sticky. No water back there. He noticed Berith watching him.

He pulled his hand out and offered the driver a stick of gum from a pack. The man shook his head 'no' and drove on.

Tyson was tired, he realized. It had been a long day and a long night. How long had it been since he'd slept? Two nights? Three?

She'd not let him sleep at all since Wednesday. Twice she got out of her ropes. Once to get out of the cabin, once to attack him. That was the beginning of the end for that task.

"Not safe out here, generally speaking. Jeff," said Berith breaking the long silence.

"How's that?"

"Lots of people disappear from reservation lands. It's a scandal."

"This one?" asked Tyson. "I mean... are we on Indian land?"

"We are," he said.

"Lots of people, huh?"

"Across the country and beyond. Canada too."

"I thought that was all done by schools." Tyson had heard something that somewhere.

"You talking about that mass grave they say they found a while back?"

"Maybe."

"That didn't happen. Media hype bullshit. No grave there, just accusations and no apologies. But individuals do go missing all the time. Usually young girls, but some young men too."

"I'm not from here," said Tyson.

"No, I figured not. But it's a problem."

"What do you think happens?"

"What do you think?" said Berith.

"Frankly, I've seen the reservations. I'd leave. Who wouldn't leave? It's better over the fence and they know it."

"Makes sense. To a point."

'To a point,' made Tyson think of his knife. He turned to hide his smirk and looked out the window. High clouds must be moving in. The stars were dimmer, not as many twinkles as before, even though all daylight was now good and gone. The moon too was a little flat.

"What brought you to the side of the road this night?" Berith asked.

"Car conked out."

"Oh? I didn't see it."

"Off on a side street. I hit something in the road, then I hit a ditch. Hard."

"What you doing on a side street?"

"Taking a shit."

"You just left your car?"

Tyson didn't like this conversation and wondered if he hadn't said too much already. If that Honda was found soon and identified, if the area was searched before the ground had settled, that might mean trouble particularly if this guy could link him to it. "It wasn't worth the cost of a tow," said Tyson. "Got it for a hundred dollars and a Big Mac back in, eh, Albuquerque."

"Sounds stolen."

"No. It was a shit beater. I left the title in the glove box. Signed it and everything for whoever finds it." It was a nice lie to make him look cool and shift the direction of the talk. "So, how about you?" he asked. "Why you driving on this lonely road?"

"Doing my route."

"A man's gotta hustle," said Tyson. "Stay one step ahead of the bastards."

"It's a jungle out there?"

"That's what I'm saying. You know what I'm talking about."

"Anything goes?"

"No, kill or be killed," said Tyson.

"That's what it means?"

"Doesn't it?" asked Tyson.

"What about higher law?" said Berith.

"What's higher than that?"

"Law law."

"Cops? Are you kidding me? Those who aren't on the take are knuckle-dragging buffoons."

"Well, cops themselves have been known to kill."

"You know why that happens?"

"I've heard theories," said Berith.

"They do it, because it's fun."

Berith turned and regarded Tyson with his dark eyes. The dim dash did little to show his expression, but Tyson saw a little nod of understanding if not agreement.

"Yeah," said Tyson, nodding himself. "You hunt?"

"I have."

"My first kill was my neighbor's dog," said Tyson. "Thing bit me. I thought it had rabies, so bang-bang-bang with my father's gun."

"Did you get rabies?"

"No. It didn't have rabies. Just a mean old bitch. My dad told the neighbors if they didn't want their dog shot, they should have locked it up."

"What kind of dog?"

"One of those Mexican yappy shits with bulgy eyes."

"The kind that used to sell tacos?"

"That's the one."

"Real dangerous breed."

"I shot a Rottweiler once too. And a Pit Bull. A couple those. A horse."

The clouds had thickened more. He couldn't see stars now, and the horizon, black and distant, was undifferentiated from the sky. All was dark and getting darker as the moon too became more obscure.

Tyson couldn't see the speedometer and had little reference around him to make a guess. No mile markers, no signs that shone, only the stripes down the center to give him any idea. He figured they were north of seventy miles per hour, which seemed slow and fast at the same time. Slow because he liked going ninety, at least, and fast because the headlights stretching out ahead of the car were weak and murky too.

"Gotta get your headlights cleaned," suggested Tyson.

"They might need it," said Berith.

It was getting warm in the car, and without asking, Tyson tapped the switch to roll his window down. It was a quaint little button, this luxury model being one of the first American cars to offer such a thing as power windows.

The air that cut in was hot and wild, smelled of smoke.

"There must be fire nearby," Tyson said as he rolled the window back up. "This wind will have a heyday with that."

"Not much to burn out here," said Berith.

"Has to be far away, or we could see the light. Can't see any light. But the smoke would explain that, and the stars."

"What about the stars?"

"Can't see them," said Tyson.

Berith leaned forward and looked up through the windshield. "I can't see any at all. Were there some before?"

"A sky full."

"Sorry I missed it."

"And a full moon, bright as a silver dollar."

"I don't see that either."

"No," agreed Tyson. "It's gone."

They fell into silence again, and Tyson imagined how he'd take out Berith. He had lots of tricks, but truth be told, he didn't feel like driving right then. Maybe the stars had aligned for Berith and today would be the day he had another day.

So tired. The damn heat in the car was getting to him.

"You got air conditioning in this?"

"It can't keep up," said Berith.

Tyson thought to open the window again but remembered what it was like out there. The heat and the long day and the lack of sleep were conspiring to make him sleepy. He thought back through the day, remembered the girl, sixteen years old? Eighteen? She'd given her clan names to him as he dragged her out of the car, like it was some kind of magic spell. Or maybe it was an Indian death ritual, remembering the family. She knew she was going to die. He didn't even pretend he wasn't going to kill her. Not since she hit him. Maybe she just wanted him to hear who she was before the end. Whatever.

It'd been sweet. Warm and thick and slow, as he liked it. After years of doing it fast, he'd finally found the speed he liked. Slow and screamy. Creamy and screamy.

He chuckled at that, yawned. Berith glanced over.

And the road sped under them.

It was a sand burial. He looked for that now. He'd actually consulted geological maps before he got here to identify such places. Had to clean up, and if it took too long, it ruined the moment. Sand was the way to go. No water though. His nails were dirty. His pocket sticky. He needed a truck stop.

As if he'd conjured it, a sign appeared up ahead, *Ciel 5 miles*.

"Ciel?" he said. "What's that?"

"I think it's French," said Berith.

"No, I mean a town? A gas station?"

"Never been."

"It's close."

"No, not so much."

Tyson thought he could sleep if it weren't for the heat. It was sliding from uncomfortable to painful. Worse, he felt it on his head.

He reached up to soothe his skull and his hand came away red and bloody. He turned away, hiding it. He must have dragged it out of his pocket. Had there been that much?

His head ached and then his vision blurred when a trickle of blood found its way past his eye lid.

He rubbed it clear, made it worse, then better. Then felt his head.

"You got a bad bump there, Tyson," said Berith.

"Must be from the crash. Was worse than I remember."

"What do you remember about it?"

"Uhm. I did my thing, then I was driving, then I hit something and went hard into a ditch, and then... and then... I was on the road. Ah, hell. I've got a concussion."

"Or worse," said Berith.

Ciel next exit.

Tyson pointed at the sign. "Hey, pull off there. I might need a doctor. At least a truck stop."

"We can't go there," said Berith.

"Why not?"

"You know why."

"What do I know? And what name did you just call me?"

"Tyson, you know that Ciel is not where we're going."

And the classic car passed the final exit to head down the other road, the ever-darkening, ever-warming, never-ending road where Tyson was eagerly awaited.

Hounded

Elizabeth Suggs

It was midnight when I stepped onto the Greyhound—destination: anywhere but home. My mind buzzed from my last bump, though my stash was thin after Mom found most of it. I had just enough left to keep the world at bay, at least until I ran out. Mom kicked me out after she found it, and I didn't blame her. She even said Zachary—my boy—was safer without me.

She wasn't wrong.

The driver kept silent as I shuffled past sleeping riders and others lost in their own worlds and settled in a seat near the window. The seats felt the same as when I was a kid, riding with Mom on day trips around the East Coast, back when we used to talk for hours. Now, we couldn't look at each other without fighting.

I stared out the window, past the flickering orange streetlights, to the pale glow of the moon, which washed over me like a soothing balm, the rumble of the engine lulling me into a tranquil daze, where the world outside faded into a blur of shadows and shimmering silver. In that haze, the lines between dreams and reality blurred. For a moment, Zachary was back in my arms, my mother in the kitchen baking cherry pie. The ache in my chest dulled, and I let myself drift.

It might have been three hours later—or maybe more—when the bus jolted violently, hitting a pothole so deep it rattled my bones. My eyes snapped open. A thin woman sat beside me wearing a doctor's mask, her posture unnervingly stiff. She stared straight ahead, not moving, not even acknowledging that I'd woken up.

"Excuse me?" My voice cracked, throat dry from hours of disuse. She didn't flinch, didn't blink.

I gave her a small tap, just in case she hadn't heard, but she didn't budge. Her body was cold and still, like a statue. I looked around the bus—empty seats everywhere.

"I really would like my own space. So, if you wouldn't mind—"

She didn't respond.

Fine. I'd move myself.

I swung my leg over her lap, careful not to touch more of her than I had to, but as I pulled my other leg across, her eyes snapped toward me. I froze. She grabbed my leg, her bony fingers digging into my skin like a vise. The stench of sweat and garbage hit my nose, and I winced, my stomach turning.

But it wasn't her touch that rattled me—it was her eyes. They were too familiar. My chest tightened. I knew those eyes.

I tore myself free, tumbling into the seat across from her, slamming my nose into the armrest. Warm blood trickled over my lips, metallic and thick. I wiped at it, then stopped. There, in the seat, sat a boy who couldn't have been older than six. Blond hair, alabaster skin, dark blue eyes. He looked exactly like Zachary.

But he wasn't Zachary.

He stared at me with a coldness that cut deep. The same coldness my son had when I left. The same hurt, the same confusion.

"You're bleeding," he said, pointing at my arm.

I glanced down. Drops of crimson had splattered the seat, but there was no wound. It was my nose—the warm trickle over my lips. I wiped it, feeling the sting of raw skin.

Then his voice, soft and low: "You should take a bump."

My heart skipped. My hand twitched toward my bag, where the kit lay tucked inside, ready to quiet the chaos. But I couldn't. Not in front of him.

"Yeah, get high," came another voice. I turned, and the woman beside me had ripped down her mask.

I recoiled. "No." My insides screamed *yes*, but I couldn't. Not here. Not like this.

She leaned closer, her voice dripping with derision. "You're on the road. No one will know."

"Everyone will know," I said, the realization hitting me hard. "Everyone always knew."

Every time I thought I could hide it—stuffing it in my mom's bathroom, sneaking into public restrooms—people always knew. They could see it in my eyes, smell it in my skin.

The boy watched me. "Yeah, so what? You're not young anymore. You've still got time. At least until some guy knocks you up with something worse."

The woman—my mother—laughed.

"Stop," I whispered, but they kept going, the voices intertwining, urging me to give in.

"You've given up on yourself," the boy said coldly. "You've given up on *me*."

I clamped my hands over my ears, blood smearing across my skin. My vision blurred, and I stumbled toward the front of the bus. I had to get off. I needed to leave. Now.

The driver didn't even look at me. The bus just kept rolling through the dark, endless road. "I need to get off this bus!"

"No can do," the driver said, voice flat.

"Why not?" I snapped. I glanced back at the woman and the boy, but they looked different now—normal. Like strangers. Had I imagined it all?

"No stops until Dayton."

Dayton. Could I really go that far? Could I leave my boy behind, just disappear into nothing?

"I need to get off," I repeated, my voice desperate now. "I need to go home."

The driver turned.

It was my face staring back at me.

"You've got to really want it," they said softly.

I stood there, trembling. My kit was still in the bag, within reach, and it would be so easy. Just one more bump and I'd be gone. Lost. Forgotten.

But I couldn't.

"I really want it to end," I whispered, barely audible.

The bus shuddered to a stop. The doors hissed open, the night air rushing in, cold and still. I didn't look back at the boy or the woman. I stepped off into the darkness, lit only by the pale moon.

It would take hours to walk back home. My shoes weren't made for this, but blisters were a small price to pay for seeing my baby again.

The Call of the Wild Road

Jonathan Reddoch

The wild road calls
    It beckons
It consumes
It devours miles and smiles

The gal at the diner sighs
"Tell me about it?"
Show, don't yell, I remind myself

The wheels of my mind grind
Countering the gears of my steed
The RPMs will not be televised

I killed a man in Fresno
Just to spread my creed
I've seen every hell, ma'am
I've been to every hell

Blood on the road
Gasoline in the air
My motor's running
And so am I

From the law
From sin
From him
The specter hunts me
Haunts me, taunts me
Always a mile ahead
A shadow behind

Buckshot

Bryan Young

The further the sun descended through the leaves and the longer the shadows grew, the more Mike worried. He clutched the wheel and kept the pedal floored, trying to remain confident in the old highway they'd taken, but he didn't want to let the others know of his discomfort. At 19, he was the oldest, and he didn't want anyone to think he was nervous. It wasn't his fault; the map on his phone led them to a road that looked like it hadn't been repaved in thirty years.

"We're lost," Gina said from the back seat. At 16, she was the youngest and, as John's little sister, they were responsible for her.

"It's like an adventure," Mike said.

John pulled his feet off the dashboard and sat upright in the passenger seat. "I don't think anybody's used this road in like a hundred years."

The remaining bright spots of sun on the pavement that managed to pierce through the trees dwindled, and Mike's stomach somersaulted with worry. He didn't like driving at night, let alone on one-lane country roads. He twisted on the headlights, brightening the stretch ahead of him, terrified he'd crash headlong into someone ahead of them.

"Where are we then, if this is an adventure and we're not lost?" Gina collapsed into the back seat. Mike spied her in the rear-view mirror and narrowed his eyes.

"Are you strapped in?"

She laid down below his gaze. "I will when we get to civilization. I'm laying down now."

"I'm not trying to be a hard ass," Mike said, "But I promised your mom I wouldn't let any harm befall you."

Gina groaned.

Johnny laughed. "She really said that, didn't she?" He adopted her tone in perfect mimicry. "'And let no harm befall her...'"

Mike couldn't help but chuckle. "Yeah, she did. But the point is, that's the only reason she let you come. And you wanted to come, right?"

"Fine," she said, and her tone made Mike feel a hundred years old.

Is this what his parents felt like?

Mike watched her sit up in the rear-view mirror and reach for the seat belt. "Thank you," he said.

"Watch it!" Johnny screamed.

Mike's heart leapt with John's scream. Without thinking, he jammed on the brakes and jerked the wheel away from the road, but that didn't stop the windshield from shattering and the airbags from exploding. Metal crunched. Blood sprayed into his face.

The car skidded to a halt.

Mike hit his head somewhere along the way. On what, he couldn't tell.

His head felt heavy.

Blood tasted thick in his mouth.

Blinking, he looked around.

The car came to a complete and screeching halt.

The air bags deflated. The windshield was a spider's web of shattered fractals, covered in blood and bile. Through the center was a series of spikes. He looked over to John who was shaking off the blow.

Mike spun in place, panicked, to see Gina. She hadn't gotten her seatbelt on, and her clothes dripped blood and gore. "Gina!"

She was awake, at least, but groggy. Not a great sign. The words "let no harm befall them" echoed in his head like a chorus. Or maybe that was just the ringing in his ears.

"Gina, look at me, I need you to focus. Are you okay?"

"Huh? Ye-yeah..." she said hesitantly. "What happened?"

John coughed, wiping blood from his face. "We hit a deer."

"What?" Mike said. That seemed impossible. He hadn't even seen it. But looking over to the windshield, he realized the spikes protruding through the windshield were antlers. The blood dripping down the windshield and spattered across the car's interior belonged to the deer. "Jesus."

Mike didn't know what to do.

He figured maybe the first thing was to get out of the car and figure out how bad the damage was. If he could drive away, that would be best. They hadn't seen anyone on the road in a while, so if they were stuck without a car that worked, it would be a big pain in the ass. Then he wondered if he'd be able to drive the car anyway because the airbags had been engaged. Would it even let him turn the engine over until that situation was fixed?

Mike didn't know. Besides, the windshield was opaque with cracks and blood. He wouldn't be able to see enough to drive.

He hated being the oldest.

He forced the door with his shoulder, and it opened with a hideous creak.

Mike staggered from his car, a little red Geo he'd gotten fourth hand, with a rebuilt engine, an a/c that barely worked at all, and a heater that worked all too well.

There were no streetlights on the road, and the moonlight seemed non-existent, so the only real light came from one smashed headlight and the car's interior when the door opened. At least the battery worked. Mike tried wiping blood from his face with his forearm but only ended up smearing it around further. He gagged at the smell of bile. When his eyes adjusted to the light, he got a full sense of the damage to his little car.

There was a deer crushing the hood.

Massive.

Five-point buck. Easy.

Or something. He didn't quite know what that meant, but he assumed it meant that's how many points it had on its antlers, and he knew that was at least how many holes it made in his windshield.

It moaned lowly and kicked at nothing in particular.

The buck was still alive.

It didn't matter that it was bleeding out, its throat was torn open, and its belly had split open from the impact of the vehicle.

Somehow, it was still alive.

The deer mewed.

Mike couldn't tell if it was asking for help or warning him away, but its bleating death scream sent a horrified shiver through him. No living thing should make a sound like that.

"Guys," he said weakly to Johnny and Gina, but he didn't know if they heard him over the deer. He said it again, louder, "Guys!"

The deer stopped. Its eyes, eerie black circles the size of saucers, stared into him. Mike saw his reflection in them. The deer's head was trapped, upside down, its horns caught in the glass. But it remained calm for a moment. Its kicking stopped.

The poor brute kept its eyes locked on Mike as he approached. He didn't know why he got closer to it, but he fell under the spell of the creature's gaze. As if it were calling him to witness its last breaths. Tentatively, Mike reached out a hand to pet the dying god. Maybe he could comfort it in its last moments as its breathing slowed further.

The passenger door bolted open, startling Mike... and the deer.

The deer screamed and bucked.

Johnny screamed too.

Mike recoiled, a jolt of adrenaline—he didn't realize he had any left after the accident—coursed through his body, He pulled his hand back to his chest and leapt backward.

The deer managed to find the strength to extricate itself from the car, pulling the entire pane of shattered safety glass with him, sending cubes of it flying in Mike's direction and others skittering onto the pavement. Mike held his forearms up, protecting his face from the new shower of glass, and took another step back away from the kicking deer, hoping he didn't catch a hoof in the face.

John fell back into the car.

The deer hit the pavement, bucking wildly, but lost the strength to continue. He collapsed to the side of the road, crunching the windshield apart as he fell.

"Holy shit," Johnny said.

In the absence of the struggle, there was a silence, and filling the low end of that silence were Gina's tears. "Gina, are you okay?"

Through sobs, she said, "I think I swallowed deer blood."

That gag started in his stomach and crept quickly up the back of his throat. He held it back and shot a hand to his mouth, forcing his own bile back down into his stomach where he hoped it would stay.

No wonder she was crying.

The deer moaned low, and the shallow up and down breathing in its chest ceased all together. Its tongue lolled from its mouth, and its eyes, so full of soul a moment ago, rolled eerily into the back of its head.

"What the hell are we supposed to do?" Johnny asked.

Naturally, as the oldest and the one with the car, that made everything Mike's problem. He was supposed to fix everything. "I'll call my dad," Mike said.

Because that would solve everything.

His dad *could* fix anything.

Mike took one last look at the damage, now that the deer had vacated the hood, and frankly, it looked brutal. It looked like he got into a head-on collision with another car. The hood was crumpled and caved, the grill was torn up and indented into a "V", and the windshield was gone where it had taken it with him.

His dad wasn't going to be able to *fix* it, and he wasn't going to like bailing him out, but he *would* bail them out.

Kneeling on the front seat, Mike went to grab his phone, but it wasn't where he'd left it. It had been in the phone holder on the dash, showing him the map... But now it was gone. It was above the level of the windshield. "Goddamn it," he said to himself. "You see where my phone went?"

Gina shook her head.

"Do you have your phone?"

But Gina shook her head again. "I don't have a phone."

What 16-year-old girl didn't have a goddamn phone?

Mike pulled his head from the car and leaned his elbows on the hood. "Johnny, gimme your phone."

John stood over the deer, his head lowered. "Huh? Oh."

Patting his pockets, John withdrew his phone and tossed it to Mike. Mike caught it, but the screen was shattered. He tried to put his thumb on it to input the security code, but the screen displayed nothing but random strips of colored lines. "It's broken, man."

"What?"

Mike tossed the phone back, and John did the same thing, testing it. "Oh, come on. Are you kidding me? This sucks."

"We'll have to find mine."

Mike went back into the car and started looking in all of the nooks and crannies, and then in the back seat, hoping that whatever concussive impact knocked the holder from the dashboard hadn't destroyed his phone, too.

Ten full minutes of searching and tearing everything out of the car yielded nothing. He found the remains of the holder but not the phone.

"Damn."

They'd have to walk to a payphone or flag down another driver. But as he thought about it, Mike couldn't think of a single car that had passed them in either direction since they'd crashed. That was unusual. When they were driving, they got passed pretty regularly.

Then he scoffed.

Who had payphones anymore?

They just needed to get a line out to Mike's dad. That's it. Once they did that, they could just sleep easy. "We've got two choices really. Or three, I guess."

"What's that?" Johnny asked. He paced around the car, probably trying to work out the nervous energy he'd built up since the accident. He kept pulling out his phone and trying to open it.

Mike blew out a long breath and ran both hands through his tangle of short, curly hair. "We split up. You two stay here, and I'll keep walking. I'll find a payphone or something. I call my dad, and he helps us find a tow truck or something. We're only five hours from home, so it won't be that big a deal."

"What're the other options?" Gina said, getting out of the car. She stretched her legs, closed the door behind her, and sat atop the trunk.

"We wait here, flag someone down for help, and hope they have a working cell phone. The third option is we split up. I give you guys the code to my phone, and you keep looking for it. If you find it, you call my dad. If you can't, you still flag down help. I go find a payphone anyway. We hedge our bets, I guess."

Johnny threw his arms in the air.

Gina shrugged.

She looked at her brother and back to Mike.

Johnny curved around to the back of the car and chopped a hand out toward his sister and pointed. "What do you want to do? You want to stay with me or go with Mike?"

She looked at them back and forth. Mike really didn't want to be responsible for her, and knowing her well enough, he couldn't imagine she wanted walk forever in the dark. It came as no surprise when she said, "I'll stay."

"If you find them, my dad's number is listed under Dad. Call him and tell him what's going on," Mike told them. "My passcode is one-nine-eight-nine."

Gina scoffed.

Johnny looked at her with confusion. "What?"

She shrugged. "I just didn't think Lover here was a Swiftie."

Mike sighed. "I'm going."

And he did.

Since he hadn't remembered passing anything close to walking distance, he set out in the direction they'd been heading. It was an old highway, so there was bound to be something eventually. Hopefully, not the Bates motel.

The beam of the headlight disappeared behind him, and he was left wondering if he were in a horror film. The crunching beneath each step made a beat of sorts for the music of the night. Crickets provided the strings. The empty silence of the night, that slow blow of the wind, added a melodious hum. The trees shed leaves in an irregular pattern, adding an unusual staccato that thrummed through the scary tune Mike walked through.

He didn't know how long the night's music lasted, but it grew more intense with every step.

The faster he walked, the faster the tempo became.

"Relax, Mike," he told himself. "We'll find something. It'll be okay. It'll be okaaay," he sang in time with the dark sounds.

But he didn't believe it.

He thought about the deer. He thought about there being more of them out there, staring at him from all directions with those terrifying black eyes, invisible in the foliage. He wondered what other animals would be out there. Bears maybe. Mountain lions? Wolves? Coyotes? Mike didn't know all that much about what sorts of animals were around exactly. He knew about the foothills around home, but this far away, he may as well have been in a tropical rain forest ten thousand miles away. There could be cheetahs and elephants for all he knew.

Some dark shadow in the back of Mike's mind made him wonder if there was something even more lethal and worrisome to consider in the darkness. Some serial killer. He knew the state prison was around somewhere, if he hadn't gotten his directions mixed up.

Mike wondered if they'd found his phone or not. He hoped they had and that his phone hadn't been shattered like John's.

He wondered how much time had passed, how long he'd been walking into the night, following the gentle curves of the highway through its upward slopes and downward valleys.

No cars passed in either direction.

No help anywhere.

It could have been two hours or five, Mike couldn't tell, but the trees parted from the road and the moon hung high in the sky, full and bright. There was more light to see by than he'd had all night, and ahead he saw a turn off the road. A building stood, though no lights heralded its existence. He recalled seeing no signs for it, either. A hundred yards ahead, he saw the vague outline of a signpost where the turn-off began, but the sign itself had been long removed.

It appeared to be a rest stop. Maybe it hadn't been used in a while, but it was a building nonetheless, which made it his first, best chance of getting help.

It took an eternity to reach the building once he saw it. His legs and eyes burned heavy with exhaustion. Maybe he'd been walking longer than he'd thought. Maybe the sun was just on the other side of the mountain's peak, just waiting to rise, and Mike had really been up all night.

The building was condemned, a haunted house in the center of a dark forest on a fall night, beaming beneath the light of a full moon.

The only thing that could make it creepier was the...

...and there it was...

The howl of a wolf in the distant hills.

Mike shuddered as he moved for the glass door. Pressing his eyes to it, he wrapped his hands around his eyes like binoculars to cut the glare. Blood red tiles covered the foyer's floor that led to gendered bathrooms in each direction. There was a vending machine more full of cobwebs than candy. And beside it...

A payphone.

There was a light above the phone's box providing the only working light inside the room, leading him to believe the phone was still connected.

He checked his pockets, and his stomach did a belly flop into an empty pool. He didn't have any change.

Taking a deep breath, he'd figure it out. He'd just call collect. That was a thing, right?

He pulled the door's handle but found it wouldn't open.

"Of course."

The damn thing was chained shut.

Mike sighed.

He looked around for something to shatter the glass with, hoping it wasn't safety glass or wired together somehow like the glass windows in the doors of his high school.

All he needed was the right rock or a branch of the right size. Maybe a brick from the parking lot. Something.

Looking around yielded nothing suitable. Going back to the glass door, he pulled his leg back and kicked, but the glass wouldn't yield beneath the sole of his shoe.

"Damn it," he shouted with every kick.

He was powerless to get in.

Help was right there.

Just through that glass.

Mike screamed and put every last bit of strength he had into his legs trying to shatter the glass, but to no avail. He turned, hoping he could put more force if he kicked the window like a mule, but that didn't work either. His shoe just bounced off like the door was bulletproof.

"Oh, come on!"

Mike turned around and banged helplessly on the door with his forearms.

He was *that* close to the phone. This felt like the worst possible scenario. Lost in the middle of nowhere, dying of exposure or something. Thirst parched his throat, and he was hungry enough to eat the candy out of that spider's nest of a vending machine. And still, the glass stopped him.

A better tool was all he needed, so he turned again to find one.

Instead, he was greeted with the barrel of a gun and the sound of it cocking.

Mike gulped and raised his hands, hoping he hadn't wet himself.

On the other side of the gun was a guy who hadn't showered in weeks, maybe months. His scraggly, gray beard looked as though he hadn't shaved in years, reaching down to his chest. He was missing teeth, wheezing with whiskey and mustard gas on his breath. His eyes pointed in slightly different directions but both vaguely toward Mike. All of the fright he'd overcome to get there in the first place returned ten-fold, crackling like lightning through his bones.

"Watchu lookin' for, sonny?" the man said.

His skin, even in the moonlight, looked leathery, as though he'd lived his entire life. His clothes were in tatters and were punctuated by occasional strips of animal fur. At first, Mike thought his hair was short, but it was long and greasy, hidden beneath a raccoon-skin cap.

"I, uh..." Mike stammered. "...just lookin' for a phone."

"Rest stop's closed, boyo."

"Yeah, but I..."

The wild man raised the gun higher, aiming it at Mike's face. Mike clenched his jaw, trying not to cry. He just wanted to call his dad. Mike bit into his tongue to keep himself from talking.

"That's right. Keep it shut."

Mike inhaled deeply through his nose, trying to stay calm. If he panicked, he knew he'd get shot.

Mike's face soured. The man's stink—gamey body odor and a decade of sweat and dreck assaulted every receptor in his nostrils.

He gagged.

"What's wrong, sonny boy?" The man smiled, revealing his blackened, broken teeth. "Smell something?"

The wild man laughed, and the smell got worse. His eyes tightened with every guffaw, and black creases of dirt appeared where wrinkles should have been.

That's when Mike cracked.

It started in his chest, like a shiver. And then it traced itself up his throat and he felt his chin tighten like the pit of a plum and quiver. Then, the tears came. "I want to go home. I just want to call my dad, okay?"

"I told you to shut it!"

The man pulled the gun back, and Mike barely saw the gun came back into his face, butt first, then everything went black.

The sun was up when Mike awoke. As he took his situation into account, he realized things had gotten worse.

Other than the concussive throb in his head, the first thing he noticed was the baking heat of the sun. The second was the rag stuffed in his mouth. It tasted old, musty, and vaguely of oil. He didn't want to know where it had come from. His wrists were bound with a sunbaked rope that twisted and creaked with every movement. It felt and sounded as though it had been left outside for ages in the rain and dried out again a hundred times before binding his wrists. Then, around his middle, a length of cord attached him to a thick, knotty tree.

Once his eyes adjusted to the sunlight, Mike saw he was about thirty yards from the rest stop, but thick, overgrown foliage covered the distance between him and the edge of the paved area. His clothes were covered in dried blood and bile. Looking around close to his right, there were vague signs of a camp.

Mike heard gentle snoring and wagered the man slept during the hot parts of the day. He probably did his hunting on the edges of day and night, and with a captive like Mike, he wanted to stay out of sight when it was most likely he would be seen.

They were hidden well. Mike could *see* the rest stop, but it was a strain to do so through the foliage. He doubted anyone at the rest stop could see him.

It was difficult to breathe without the use of his mouth, and his nose felt broken.

He didn't know if he had any water left in his body to cry. He felt so dried out and hollow. Hungry and thirsty all at once. The oily rag soaked up all of his spit, and he just wanted a sip of water. Maybe that was how he could focus on his survival. Just one step at a time. If he wanted to get home, it would start with getting out of his captivity and just getting one, single sip of water.

Mike started by working the rope at his wrists. If he could get his hands free, he might be able to escape while the wild man slept. As long as he was quiet about it.

But a noise in the distance stopped him.

The bass rumble of car tires on pavement.

Mike's eyes widened.

He adjusted, trying to see if he could spot the car as the sound neared. Then he looked back in the direction of the snoring but realized it had disappeared. Whether the wild man had adjusted his position or was up and investigating, Mike couldn't tell.

Mike just wanted whoever had driven by to help him. There wasn't much he could do for himself, tied up as he was, but he had to try.

Through the leaves, he saw the car was white. But then from a different angle, it was black.

Highway patrol?

There was no way he could have gotten that lucky overnight. Ever since they'd hit that buck, Mike's luck had been awful, and he didn't expect it to have turned that quickly.

A car door opened, and indistinct voices chattered. Maybe a couple of cops? Mike couldn't tell what they said, but they were looking around. Through the shrubs and leaves, he couldn't see them, but he was able to get a better look at the car. The words "FOREST SERVICE" emblazoned on the side told the story. Maybe they could help? Maybe Johnny and Gina found his phone.

Mike's heart leapt at the thought, but it settled back down, sinking into that pit of tar in his chest when he realized they could have just been checking on the rest stop.

Mike's level of panic rose like a tide, ready to drown him until he did *something*. He wasn't sure what. The binds around his wrist weren't loosening. He couldn't get his hands up high enough to get the gag out of his mouth to call for help. He thought his muffled screams might be heard, but the risk was too high. What would happen if they couldn't hear him but the wild man did?

Options floated by him, carried on waves of uncertainty. One of the rangers stooped down low by the car. They examined the ground and pointed in Mike's direction. It looked like, for just a second, they looked right at him.

Mike didn't have a choice.

He had to risk it.

He screamed.

As loud as he could.

Right through the gag.

It felt like dragging his voice through nails and shattered glass, dry and hoarse.

He couldn't tell if they heard him or if he'd woken the wild man, but he knew his course was set.

He was escaping now and getting the help he needed or would die trying.

The rope burned at his wrists, and his fingers went numb, but he twisted and turned. But there... His wrists were free!

He loosened the cords enough to reach his mouth and withdrew the gag. His mouth felt dry like the sands of the Sahara. He took in a deep breath to bellow, but the sound of that shotgun racking back into place stopped him.

"Do it, sonny," the wild man whispered from behind. "I dare ya."

Mike paused, trying to decide.

If the wild man was going to shoot him anyway, what was there to lose? At least if he did it while the rangers were there, they'd catch his murderer.

Mike ducked to the ground and rolled. The shotgun sounded over his head, deafening him. He scrambled to his feet and screamed. "Help!"

But it came out ragged across his throat.

He coughed, staggering.

"God damn it," the wild man yelled.

The shotgun pumped and blasted once more.

Mike didn't feel it at first. He just thought he'd staggered forward. Then he realized he couldn't feel his legs. Blood was everywhere. Not just the dried blood from the deer, but his own blood. Looking down, the backs of his legs were oozing in a dozen places where the buckshot tagged him.

He grit his teeth and army crawled on his arms the rest of the way to the pavement, dragging his bloody legs behind him.

When he crested the foliage, he raised a hand and tried to yell not to shoot.

The forest service folks raised their guns and aimed them at Mike. It took a moment for them to realize he was no threat. One moved right past him and gave pursuit of the fleeing wild man, howling like a wolf into the deep forest. The other ranger came to render aid.

She holstered her gun and knelt beside him. "You Michael Bashir?"

Michael groaned in acknowledgment. "Uh-huh."

"We've been looking all night and morning for you. Your friends called it in."

But Mike didn't remember much more beyond that.

There were swirling lights.

An ambulance.

White sheets somewhere.

The smell of antiseptic.

The great mule kick of what someone said was morphine.

He was told they shot the wild man down.

But he would carry the memory of the horrors of that night forever every time he walked, limping with the wounds of that shotgun blast.

Every time he heard his feet shuffle on the pavement. Every time he heard the song of a cricket in the wind. Every time he felt the oncoming sharpness of that first autumn cold, his legs hurt the worst, and he was transported right there, back to that time.

And the eyes of the wild man.

Staring at him.

He saw those whenever he closed his eyes or when his legs hurt too badly.

As Mike grew older, he found it stunning how much one night of terror could stay inside his body just like some of those beads of buckshot, causing problems for as long as he would live.

In later years, Gina assured him it was like that for everyone and every sort of terror. Everyone had some sort of buckshot inside them, literal or figurative. Some of it just didn't come with stories as colorful as Mike's.

That's why he liked her—how they'd managed to develop a relationship years after that road trip.

She had a way of putting things into perspective for him, and she could understand, more than almost anyone, what that night was like. She had a lot of her own proverbial buckshot, too.

But that didn't stop the nightmares.

Every so often, Mike would wake up in a cold sweat with that mustard gas breath in his face. "Watchu lookin' for there, sonny?"

That shotgun would cock.

And the buckshot would hurt all over again.

Fishing the Pickling Sea

Amelia Gorman

D id I ever tell you about the time
      we caught one that big? Sawed out
a great circle in the salt. Brought
our rods and reels and made an evening
of it after the UV wasn't quite so Ultra.You touched my face gentle
where the moles
    were already starting to form and we bonded
    there like the encyclopedia says they used to
    on the ice, in the arctic. Pretend it's nice.
    Pretend it's cold. Pretend it's that big
    and still alive. But the thing you haul out isn't.Pretend we didn't
cook it on the roof of your old dodge
    The thing whose shape haunts me
    just outside my vision. The thing we ate
    choking on the bones that there this big
    and seasoned with toxicity. After all,
    we eat Aunt Cat's pickled tongue and never asked

once where the brine was from, or the tongue. I kiss

your salt-blind eyelids before night and

promise I will never share with you the shape

but only the taste. The mutability and change

catching Transformation herself on the hook.Knowing the law said
to catch & release,

but we catch and keep and consume.

Burial of Broken Vows

Melissa Pierce

The population of Murrock dried up the same way the gold did. Past its initial flourish, it waned over the late 1800s, through the advent of electricity and transcontinental railroads; through a world war and man's first flight; through a depression, another war, an assassination; until finally, by 1950, nothing and nobody was left, save for a single dusty road lined with empty structures.

'Least, it appears that way today.

There's unfinished business in Murrock. Keener tourists feel it in the sway of the rusted schoolyard swings, the whispers in the old courthouse, the breeze through the gallows. The last of the townspeople may have left when the schoolhouse closed, but there's a lingering disturbance in their wake—something already buried beneath these ruins, yet begging to be laid to rest.

"That's it! That's the shot."

Garrett hopped from foot to foot as he scrolled through the photos on his camera. "Yup. That was definitely the one," he told me. "Portfolio, complete."

I held back a sigh as I tightened my focus on the tombstone in front of me. Our photography class had been given a variety of assignments for our day in Murrock—a commercial shot, a conceptual shot, a series of similar subjects, and so on—and with the sun setting behind me, I still didn't have an abstract shot I was pleased with.

Admittedly, I had only myself to blame. The entire day trip had been a photographer's paradise. Murrock was an isolated ghost town buried deep in the hills of rural Utah, its thirty-one buildings protected and preserved as a state park, remarkably unscarred by tourism. There were no power lines to dodge, no distractions on the horizon, no modern objects lying around to spoil the aesthetic. It was flawlessly vintage. Effortlessly creepy. Visually unique, and wildly captivating. We'd had free range of the town all day, our class of forty crawling in and out of the decaying structures to capture hundreds of photos for our portfolios—photos we'd brag about later in our blog posts, knowing full well it was the subject matter, not our amateur photography skills, that took the shots from mediocre to breathtaking.

Thus why it was all the more frustrating that I didn't have a decent abstract shot yet. The only requirement was to "provide a unique perspective on an object or objects," and I'd already encountered hundreds of interesting objects throughout the day. But my shot of the door hinges in the sheriff's house felt uninspired, the abandoned truck was clearly overdone, and my close-up of the hanging ropes in the gallows felt cliché.

Now, we were in the cemetery five miles outside of town—a quick stop on our route back to the hotel for some last-minute pictures.

My shots of the crumbling tombstones were worse than anything I'd taken in the town. Golden hour was ending, and I needed to think of something. Fast.

Garrett, on the other hand, was taking a victory lap. "I can't wait to blog this! Especially my ghost photo. That'll get some attention, don't you think?"

"Uh-huh," I agreed, scanning the cemetery for a better subject. There were tombstones, and there was brush. I was going to have to get creative.

"Maybe even some ghost hunters will reach out. Don't you think? I mean, it's *right* there in the picture."

"Yeah. Could happen."

Our conversation caught the attention of two women on their way back to the bus, Marie and Ashley. "You're the one with the ghost picture?" Marie asked Garrett.

"Yeah!"

"Can we see?"

I wandered off as Garrett pulled up the photo on his viewfinder for them. I'd already seen and studied the picture myself. It was a macro shot of a shiny doorknob, with the doorknob taking up only the right third of the frame. Garrett's reflection was in the doorknob, but behind him, there was another figure standing on the road, and he swore up and down that the entire rest of the photo group had been inside the hotel at that moment. The photo was backlit, so both Garrett and the other figure were only dark outlines, and it was impossible to say who the other person was, whether ghost or human. But when we'd shown the photo to one of the park employees, she was unsurprised.

"I can't say exactly who that is," she said, "but that's certainly not the first ghost picture we've gotten in this town."

She went on to spin us a scattered tale of town lore: the hotel had once briefly been used as an infirmary, and now children's cries often echoed there; pleading had been heard in the direction of the gallows, for obvious reasons; and a man, hanged after being suspected of murdering the sheriff's daughter, was frequently sighted around the town.

"Does the man carry something with him?" asked Garrett. "It looks like this person is holding something tall and skinny in the picture. No one in our group has anything like that, except for tripods, and they aren't as tall as what this guy has."

The employee gave an exaggerated shrug. "Not that I know of. Could be him, though! I wouldn't doubt it."

The ghost picture was pretty cool, I'll admit. But it also meant that even in an *active ghost town,* I hadn't managed to get a simple abstract shot yet, and that needed to change. Now.

I wandered all the way to the far corner of the cemetery, searching for something— anything—that stood out. The tombstones were disappointingly plain and small—they must not have found much gold in Murrock after all—and they stood in wavy rows, some clumped together, some isolated. It had a haphazard feel that creeped me out the same way a black widow's messy web did—like death was imminent, so why take any care in the details?

I got to the very last grave and, realizing that this was my only remaining choice for subject matter, set about finding a unique perspective to shoot it from. Almost immediately I thought, if we so often look *down* on tombstones, why not take a shot looking *up* at one?

The idea wasn't groundbreaking, but with the sun now below the horizon, it was good enough for me.

I first tried lying on my stomach to take photos of the tombstone. When that angle didn't satisfy me, I found a stick and used it to dig a small divot in the ground. I set my camera inside it, angled it up at the grave, and pressed the shutter button over and over. I lifted my dirty camera close to my face to inspect the photos.

Presto! At long last, my abstract shot was complete. It wasn't my favorite photo I'd ever taken, but it would do. It had to.

I looked up to realize that the cemetery had emptied out since I'd been lost in my photoshoot. I looped my camera's strap over my neck and darted between the graves, racing down the hill to the road, my heart beating faster as the utter silence and still air fell over me. I approached the road, looking left and right, but there was nothing and no one.

The bus had left without me.

I squinted down the road. There wasn't a car to be seen amongst the rolling hills. Nothing back the other way, either, and no one from my class in sight.

I swallowed as the reality of the situation set in. "Stick with the group" had been a refrain throughout the trip, and my brief failure to do so had cost me. The cemetery was a good five miles away from the town, which was surely now empty, and the next spot of civilization was no closer than a two-hour drive away. I had absolutely nothing on me except my camera; everything else, including my phone, was on the bus.

I was stranded.

The sky faded from yellow to purple to black as I sat by the road, hoping madly that there was at least one straggler left in the town, one employee who would drive past the cemetery on their way home. Or maybe the photo group would realize I was gone, and the bus would come back for me.

In the meantime, there was nothing to do but wait.

It was unnerving to be so completely alone. I was tempted to distract myself by looking through the photos on my camera but decided instead to save the battery; I could use the flash as a flashlight if I needed to. There was a mere half-moon to break up the darkness, though I was lucky that it was warm and clear. Crickets chirping and a crow cawing were the only signs of wildlife. Even so, I decided it was best not to sleep the hours away. I needed to keep an eye out for cars, and really, what did I know about this land? Anything could be lurking in the distance.

I'd only been waiting a short while when I heard a sound. Was it an animal? No, it was too sharp, too regular. A shovel striking dirt, coming from behind me. I checked the road once more—no one in sight—and quickly made up my mind. I would give anything to avoid spending the entire night alone in the wilderness accompanied only by dilapidated graves.

I scrambled back up to the cemetery. "Hello? Hello!"

At first, I didn't see anyone. But as I moved over the crest of the hill, I spotted a person near the back of the graveyard, digging into the tough soil. "Hey!" I called out.

The person didn't seem to hear me, so I ran toward them. "Hey! Excuse me—do you have a phone?"

Still no response. I ran faster until I could see that it was a man who held the shovel. He was illuminated by a weak lantern, and I quickly realized the lantern wasn't the only antiquated thing about him. He was wearing a ragged coat with a vest and collared shirt underneath and a western hat I'd seen only in old films. His facial hair was long and haggard.

He had to have heard me running, but he didn't stop digging to look up, even when I was only ten feet away. "Excuse me?" I said gently. "Sir?"

It was like I didn't exist. The man struck the shovel into the ground mechanically, over and over, into a hole that was already a couple feet deep, his pace rapid but unhurried. I noted the caked dirt on his skin, the patched holes in his coat, the worn shoes, and the tied handkerchief on the ground beside him, realizing with a sinking feeling that there wasn't a chance in hell this man had an iPhone in his pocket. This was either a homeless man in a suit or a western reenactor taking their role too seriously. Regardless, I realized, he was my only chance at finding a way home.

I took just one step closer, and now I pleaded. "Sir, please... I missed my bus. I need to find somewhere with a phone so I can call my tour group. We were just here to take photos for the day." I raised my camera as proof. "I would really, really appreciate your help. I don't know what else to do."

The man finally stopped digging, but as soon as he looked up at me, my stomach sank.

Desperate as I was, I regretted getting his attention. The man looked absolutely wrecked with grief. The skin underneath his eyes was grayed. His eyes were piercing, almost accusatory, and I was now directly in their path.

"She's my girl," he said, his voice low and groggy. "You understand."

A chill went through me as he acknowledged me directly. His accent was old and western, not of this time, not like a reenactor's. "P-pardon?"

He rested the tip of the shovel on the ground, hanging his head. It was only then, as my eyes explored what was lit by the dim glow of the lantern, that I noticed the tombstone he was staring at, so old it was half-sunken into the ground.

Caroline Ward

died March 3, 1864

aged 19 years

The man sniffled loudly, making me jump back from the tombstone. He looked right at me again, shame clouding his eyes. "I miss 'er too much. I just... have to..."

Dread seeped into my stomach as my imagination scrambled to finish his sentence. "Have to... what?" I asked.

He pried his eyes away from me, and slowly, guiltily, the man raised his arm to point directly in front of him at the tombstone of Caroline Ward and the gaping hole in front of it.

"I know it's wrong," he said, his voice pitching up in grief, "but I need 'er back."

He nodded to himself. And then, with conviction, he struck the shovel into the ground again, and he continued to unearth the grave of the dead woman.

This couldn't be real. I stepped back, blinking hard, but the image of the man never wavered. Briefly, I entertained the thought that he might be a ghost—but could a ghost wield a shovel, move dirt? I thought of touching the dirt pile beside the man but couldn't make myself take one step closer. I didn't want to be anywhere near here when he reached the coffin. I began to back away slowly.

"Say—"

I nearly jumped out of my skin. The man was staring at me again—this time, at the camera hanging around my neck. He pointed at it with a shaky hand.

"You want my camera?" I held it up. He could have anything he wanted if it meant I got back to the road unscathed.

But the man ignored my question. "You're the... photographer."

His tone lilted up at the end of his statement, like he was hopeful, so I nodded, not wanting to risk disappointing him. "Yeah, I am."

The man nodded, starting to smile. "You're here for our weddin' day."

"You and—Caroline?"

The man grinned. His teeth were twisted in all directions. "My beautiful bride-to-be," he said, gazing at the grave. "Been too long we've been engaged. We made a promise at the crick... Some said I was a fool for askin' 'er. But she said yes. Was only days before the weddin' when..."

His face clouded over. I froze with fear, but when the man looked back at me, his face was hopeful again. "But the pictures! They'll all see our weddin' day, and they'll know she's been mine all along. And we'll smile big, don't you worry now. We won't even blink."

As if to prove it, the man froze in place. He stayed eerily unmoving, unblinking, not even seeming to breathe as he stared at me, like a wax figure posing with a shovel.

I realized he was waiting for my confirmation, but I'd become so paralyzed with fright it took me nearly ten seconds to respond. "...Yes. Okay, yes. I'll take your pictures."

The man jerked a sudden nod, and then he was back to digging, with no seeming transition between the movements. One second he was staring at me, the next his head was tilting down, and the next he was back in the hole, halfway through a shovel of dirt.

Thoroughly shaken, I silently backed away from the man, hoping he was too entrenched in his task to notice. But I hardly got a few steps away before I noticed the digging had stopped. The man was standing next to the hole, shovel in hand, glaring furiously at me.

"The photographer," he growled stubbornly.

"Yes!" I put my hands up and moved back toward the hole. "Yes. I'm the photographer."

The man returned to digging.

I took a deep breath. Staying here wasn't an option. I needed to be back at the road in case the bus came back, not waiting for this man—mortal or otherwise—to successfully unearth his dead fiancée, and the hole looked at least half-dug already. There was nowhere to hide in the scrub brush-speckled hills, but I'd rather attempt to outrun this man forever than witness whatever was coming next.

I waited until the man's head was bent low, and this time, I broke out in a dead sprint toward the road.

Immediately, there were footsteps behind me. I ran faster, breathed harder, flying between the uneven tombstones. Before long, I had to look down to avoid tripping over a tumbleweed, and when I looked back up, I came to a stumbling halt. The man was miraculously, impossibly, in front of me, face bent in anger, shovel pointed threateningly.

"*The photographer.*"

My mouth hung open as I raised my hands in surrender once again. This man may have looked like he'd stepped straight out of the 1800s, but he was taller than me, faster than me, and armed with a shovel he looked all but eager to use against me.

Numbly, I nodded my consent—"Y-yes, I'm the photographer"—and let him march me back to Caroline's grave.

I waited obediently as the man returned to digging, raking my fingers down the neck strap of my camera, intensely regretting my choice to have ever left the roadside. I was in much deeper than I'd thought. This man was not going to let me out of his web until he had what he wanted from me. My safest option was to just take the pictures, hope the man was satisfied, return to the road, and get picked up by morning. I dreaded my plan, but I couldn't see any way around it. My only hope was that it would all be over quickly.

At that very moment, I heard the dull thump of metal against wood, followed by a deep groan.

I snapped my attention back to the gravesite. Somehow, the man was already standing in a neck-deep hole, all sides carved straight down to Caroline's coffin. "I got 'er!" he said, thunking the shovel against the wooden lid again. "Oh, don't worry, Caroline, I got 'cha..." He jerked his head up to find me. "Photographer! Grab that lantern, will ya? And shine it on over us?"

I stepped terrifyingly close to the grave, picking up the handle of the lantern that was very much solid, stepping next to the loose dirt pile that looked very much real. This was happening. I held the lantern over the hole, careful not to look down. "This good?"

"That'll do."

I stared at the dark horizon, trying not to shake as I listened to him wrestle with the wooden lid of the coffin. "C'mon on, now, Caroline, don't be testy..."

I heard the splintering of wood, squeaking hinges, and creaking, groaning, grinding as the man pried open the coffin's lid. And then there was an unearthly howl—half-animal, half-human—as the man laid eyes on the remains of his fiancée.

"Oh, Caroline!" he said, his voice teary. "She's beautiful. Just same as the day I met her. Oh, photographer, won't you take a photograph of my beautiful bride? C'mon, now. Take a picture of my sweet, sweet Caroline..."

It took everything in me to pry my eyes from the horizon and look down into the grave. The man was bent over Caroline's scattered skeleton, stroking her skull, the box around them warped and ravaged. His adoration might have been sweet under vastly different circumstances. He smiled proudly up at me. "Take the picture, and they'll see. They'll see we were always meant to be together..."

I took a deep breath, shaking the jitter out of my hands. This was almost over. I raised the camera to my eye, preparing to point it at the horrifying scene. But then I noticed something.

"What's that?" I asked, pointing at the deep scratch marks on the inside of the coffin's lid.

The man followed my finger, his expression darkening at the destination. "That's none..." He grumbled, shifting to face me again. "None 'ya concern. Take the photo, son."

I squinted in the dark. The scratch marks were definitely real, and they looked old, old as the coffin itself. I looked back at the man, who was clearly growing uncomfortable, and felt a slow churning in my stomach. As I looked back down to Caroline, my eyes caught on a circling lump beneath his shirt collar. One shirt button had come undone in his digging, and now, barely visible, was a loose loop of rope around his neck.

Everything clicked into place, sending a burst of righteous adrenaline through me. "You're the man who was hanged for murdering the sheriff's daughter! You *killed* Caroline!"

The words were out of my mouth before I'd decided to say them. The man leapt out of the grave so fast he seemed to phase there—in the hole one second, on the ground the next—and then he was stalking toward me as fast as I could back up. I stumbled over myself, trying frantically not to trip, regret and panic overwhelming me.

"You ALL say I killed Caroline!" he yelled, gripping the shovel over his head with both gloved hands. "But I'm an innocent man! She was neckin' with a traveler. Had a wanderin' eye—whole town knew it! And so I buried 'er beneath the ground—livin'!—'till I could have 'er to myself. *I was comin' back for 'er!*"

He shook his head angrily, finally coming to a stop. I struggled to keep my grasp on the lantern as I shuddered in terror, feeling only the slightest relief when he lowered the shovel, still shaking his head as he spoke. "But the sheriff noticed... 'fore I knew it, the whole town was after me. Sayin' I killed my sweetheart. Sayin' she was never true to me, and I retaliated for it." His voice lowered. "They got to me 'fore I got to 'er. And so I died, and so did she. That was the joke of it—by killin' me, they killed their only clue to Caroline."

"But—her tombstone. How did they bury her if she was already...?"

"Oh, they found 'er." The man glowered at me, as if I were the one responsible for this affront. "Took many years, but they found 'er. Reburied 'er right along with the rest of the town. But, see, I'm *through* sharin' Caroline. So, we'll finally marry, you'll take these pictures, and I'll prove she's true to me. I'll move Caroline somewhere's we can be alone together, and I'll have 'er to myself, for all of eternity. It's a man's right, to have his wife."

Nausea seized in my stomach. This man was no grieving widower come to profess his undying love; he was a monster beyond anything I could have imagined. To stay and comply as his wedding photographer now felt unbearably foolish. Why would his demands stop at taking the pictures? And at the end of it all, what could possibly motivate such a corrupt man to let the only witness of his crime run free?

I tried to take solace in the confirmation that this man was definitely a ghost; surely, this would inhibit his ability to harm me, wouldn't it?

But I didn't have the luxury of taking time to decide. "I *really*... I have to go," I chanced, taking a tiny step backward.

The man's face reddened, his eyes tightening fiercely. "You leave here now..." he warned, "you'll regret it."

I swallowed. "I'm sorry..."

His frown deepened. "'Suppose you know my feelings towards those who break promises."

I reminded myself that I had no other choice. *I had no other choice.*

With the man's eyes on my every move, I attempted to set the lantern gently on the ground, but my shaking hands flung it over on its side. I righted it in a flash, only to realize that I hadn't nearly started a fire. The lantern was lit by an electric bulb inside, not a flame. It was battery-powered.

A prop. The lantern was a prop my class had brought for the excursion and apparently left behind in the cemetery.

New thoughts raced through my mind. Was this why the man had asked me to lift it? Was he incapable of manipulating earthly objects? Had everything else he'd touched been an illusion—the shovel, the dirt, the coffin? Did he have no real ability to hurt me after all?

It was time to find out.

I held my breath as I took a step toward the road. The man stared at me, but he didn't move.

Another step. Nothing.

I turned my back on the man and ran toward the road, listening for footsteps behind me. There were none. Perhaps he'd noted the realization on my face; perhaps he'd realized that by running a third time, I was calling his bluff. Either way, I'd won. I'd won! I would live to tell this tale yet—a tale no one, not even Joshua, would believe.

But then footsteps came up sharply. I whipped around to find the man running only a few steps behind me, shovel raised. Instinctively, I flew to defend myself—against a ghost? How?—and realized that light, a bright and sudden light, was my best weapon. I raised my camera and turned on the flash.

CLICK!

For a moment, I could see everything: the man, not a foot from me now, his face twisted in rage. The damning rope around his neck. The bruising underneath his beard. His shovel raised to the sky, its blade hovering threateningly over my head.

And then the world went dark again, and darker still as I felt an intense pain in my skull, losing consciousness before I hit the ground.

When the tour group returns hours later, there's only a camera to be found in the cemetery.

It's confirmed to be the missing photographer's quickly, on account of the photos stored inside it. Plenty of door hinge photos, and there's the truck, the gallows. There are photos of graves—in particular, low-angled shots taken of an Arthur Dyer's tombstone from the far corner of the yard, died March 5, 1864.

But it's the last photos they puzzle over. Who is this man, so angry and wielding a shovel? And what are these blurry wedding photos of the same man, with a young and frightened bride on his arm?

Photographers tend to rely on their eyes, and that's what the group does tonight; all are trained tightly on the found camera. But in the dark, across the cemetery, two mounds of dirt sit piled high: one in front of Caroline's tombstone and another off to the side. Only the keenest of ears could hear the faint pleas and scratches from six feet below, begging for finality.

Hotel Regal

Brian B. Baker

The Hotel Regal sat on a nearly empty lot. It was barely a hotel and hadn't been regal in a century.

Its guests milled about, unaware of where they were. Uncertain of how long they'd stayed, there was a difference between them. They saw each other, talked to one another, and waited. They would not have to wait long for the next guest to arrive.

Tom and Mildred pulled up to the Regal. Tom booked the hotel through a website from a friend months ago. The friend was hit by a car a day later. Tom thought that was odd but kept the booking. It would be their fiftieth wedding anniversary, and he wanted them to have a good time.

Stairs led up from the street to the hotel, and while it sat back from the road on a near-empty lot, it appeared fresh and new to Tom and Mildred. It was the way the hotel worked.

"This looks nice," Mildred said, grabbing her bag from the trunk.

Tom smiled and hoped for a good night.

They hurried into the hotel as the rain pattered the ground around them. It would be the rain they remembered later and the sound it made striking the cement.

Tom hauled their bags through the front doors and stared up. A recreation of Dante's trip through hell covered the entire ceiling with little notes underneath.

"That's a bit creepy," Mildred said.

"It's not meant to be," a voice said, and they stared from the ceiling to the desk. Tom hadn't seen anyone behind the desk when they'd walked in, but now as he struggled with their luggage, a woman in a long white dress stood behind the counter.

Startled by her voice, Tom could only stare, "Oh, sorry. We have a booking for a couple of nights."

The woman brushed her blond hair from her shoulders and pulled a key from underneath the desk.

"The Millers," she said.

"Yes, Tom and Mildred," Tom said.

"I am Victoria. Welcome to the Hotel Regal," she said.

"Are there any other guests in the hotel?" Mildred asked.

"There are, but they're swamped, and you probably won't see them," Victoria replied.

"That's too bad. I like to talk to others while we're on trips. It helps pass the time."

"I understand. Well, you are certainly welcome to look around the hotel while you're here. It's over a century old, and some places have that feel to them, but as for guests, as I said, you may not see them."

"What else is there to the hotel?"

"There is a stable in the back of the grounds if you want to go horseback riding. There is a lemon orchard, but sadly it's been unable to grow fruit recently, and we haven't figured out why."

"That's too bad. I would like to see a lemon orchard. We're from Utah; this is our first time out of the state. We used to travel a lot but kept to the country's interior. Tom found this place through a friend, and tomorrow is our fiftieth wedding anniversary."

"That's wonderful to hear. I love it when people who've lived a long, happy life stay with us."

Tom and Mildred stared at Victoria.

"It was happy, wasn't it?"

"That's a bit personal for my tastes," Mildred said.

"I understand," Victoria said and passed the key to Tom. "The dining room will be open for dinner from six to ten. It will close until six in the morning when breakfast is served."

"What is on the menu?" Tom asked.

"The usual southern food," Victoria said.

"Oh, I love southern food," Mildred said.

Tom stared at her as if worms sprouted from her head, then the thought of the worms squiggling through her head appeared in his mind. He shook it off and stared at Mildred. The worms crawled from her eye sockets to her nose and mouth. Tom looked away to Victoria.

A ghastly smile adorned her face, but that was all the way there, the smile. Eye sockets filled with fire stared back at him.

Mildred touched his shoulder, and he shrugged her off, stumbled away into the wall, and looked at his wife.

The worms were gone, and it was only Mildred. Her grey hair was done up the way it had been when they arrived.

"Tommy, are you okay?" she asked.

He stared at Dante above him and then at Victoria.

"I don't know what came over me," he said.

"It's fine. The old place does that to some people their first time here. I will have someone bring you some water for your room."

Tom nodded.

A small, rickety, open brass elevator stood next to the front desk, and a set of wooden stairs lay to the left of the elevator.

"Does the elevator work?"

"Oh, yes. It works perfectly fine," Victoria said and rang a bell on the desk.

A short man with black hair and a slight hunch appeared from an open door behind her.

Tom saw a small office with a typewriter, of all things. The faint odor of cigar smoke wafted through the room.

"I am Dennis. I will take your luggage to your room. Please enter the elevator, and we will be on our way," the man said.

Tom and Mildred entered the brass elevator with Dennis, who closed the cage. A gust of cold air accompanied them into the elevator, and Tom shrugged off what he believed he'd seen of Victoria and his wife.

"Where are you from?" Dennis asked, using a handle to make the elevator move.

"Utah," Tom said. "It's been years since I've seen a hand-operated elevator."

"We like to keep things as they were made at the Regal. It's why we've been in operation for over a hundred years."

"I see that you haven't upgraded anything in the place. I saw a typewriter in the office."

"Oh yes, that. Well, for some reason, things don't work well in the Regal. Electronics go on the fritz. It isn't very reassuring. We've had electricians try to fix it, but we have to write things up on the typewriter."

"Interesting. What else goes on the fritz, as you say?"

"Phones mostly, but we've had guests who experience other electrical issues. Sometimes the lights in the room flicker, things like that. It's nothing to worry about, though."

The elevator stopped with a lurch, and Tom wasn't sure he'd seen Dennis stop it; it only appeared to control itself.

Dennis smiled and waved them out of the elevator.

"There are three floors in the Hotel Regal. With only a few guests, we wanted you on the third floor. It gives a great view of the ocean, the orchard, and the stables. I'm sure you'll enjoy it."

Dennis led them down the hallway to the door with the number fourteen on it. Tom glanced around and did not see a thirteen, only a ten and eleven.

"We don't have a number thirteen room. It's superstition, but we've kept to that through the years."

"But wouldn't this be thirteen if you were?" Mildred asked.

"I assume so, but we keep it as fourteen. It's just an old custom."

Tom nodded and handed Dennis the room key.

The door opened on a room that was far bigger than he expected.

"This isn't the room we booked," Tom said.

"It's our largest room, and we're giving it to you for your anniversary and no extra charge. Their hotel is sparsely booked, and we wanted to ensure your anniversary was special." Dennis said, and Mildred beamed.

A crystal chandelier hung in the middle of the room. Red curtains adorned the windows, which took up most of one side of the room.

"The view, as I said, overlooks the property and the ocean below the cliffs. We want the both of you to be comfortable in your new space," Dennis said.

Mildred went to the window and pulled it up. Salt, brine, and lemons wafted in the air, and she smiled as waves crashed on the rocks below.

"It's perfect," she said.

Tom smiled and handed Dennis a ten. "Thank you."

Dennis smiled and tucked the money into his pocket.

"I will leave the two of you to rest. I'm sure Victoria told you about dinner and the dining room. Once it closes, there will be no food served until morning, so make sure you come down," Dennis said, set the key on the dresser, and closed the door.

"Oh, Tommy, it's perfect. It reminds me of that little hotel we stayed at in Arizona on our honeymoon."

Tom hadn't thought of that little hotel in years. He'd barely been able to afford it, but Mildred had been unaware of that. He pulled his phone from his pocket and stared at it for a minute.

"I wonder if there is Wi-Fi?" he said.

"I doubt it; besides I don't want to sit in the hotel and stare at our phones. It's the first vacation we've had in a while. I want to go and explore that little town we passed."

"Right, you mentioned looking at the antique shops."

"Yes, there were a few of them," Mildred replied.

"It's weird to see things we grew up with considered antiques. What does that make us?"

"Antiques," Mildred replied with a smile.

Tom frowned and stared out the window.

They lay on the bed, Tom set the alarm on his phone, and they fell asleep.

The bed thumped, and Tom propped himself up and stared at it. Mildred lay asleep. Nothing ever disturbed her sleep, but what felt like someone hitting the bed from underneath he would wake her up.

Tom slipped off the bed, got on his hands and knees, and stared under the bed. Nothing, but the assault continued.

"Tommy, why are you doing that?" Mildred said.

He stood up, and she stared at him.

"I'm not doing it," he said as whatever it was slammed the mattress from underneath.

Mildred hurriedly climbed off the bed and stared at the rising and falling of it.

"What is it?" she asked.

"I don't know," he said as a knock came on the door.

Tom opened it, and Dennis stood outside the door, "Wanted to check on you. Heard some loud noises and wanted to ensure everything was okay."

Tom turned around, and the bed was still. "Yeah, we're okay, but—"

"We're fine. Nothing to worry about." Mildred said.

"The dining room will open in an hour," Dennis said and closed the door.

Tom turned to Mildred, "Why didn't you let me say anything?"

"They'll think we're crazy. Beds don't do that."

Tom sighed and nodded as he'd done numerous times during their relationship.

"We better get dressed for dinner," Mildred said.

"It's just a small dining room. It's not like we're on a cruise ship."

The horn went off, and they stared at each other.

"You were saying?" Tom said.

Mildred ran to the window, and the cliffs were gone, replaced with wave after wave of water.

"We're um—"

"We're what?"

"I don't know," she said, and Tom stepped to the window.

Water flowed beneath the window, and some splashed up and through the window.

Tom backed away, not wanting it to touch him.

"What the hell?"

Tom opened their room's door, walked to the balcony overlooking the front desk, and stared. The front doors were still there, and he saw their car beyond.

He returned to the room, walked to the window, and stared down the side of the hotel to the cliffs below.

"It's gone," he said.

Mildred opened the window and stared at the waves crashing on the rocks below, "But—"

"I don't know," Tom said, interrupting her, "but let's get ready for dinner."

They went through their rituals of preparation. Mildred took her time in the shower while Tom got his nice clothes out. He didn't want to risk being underdressed.

Mildred's dress lay on the bed, her shoes and stockings on the floor underneath the hem of the dress.

Tom stood in the room listening to the water in the shower and glanced at the clock. She'd been in there for fifteen minutes, which was longer than her usual time, "Milly, you okay in there?"

The water continued to come out of the nozzle, but there was no response.

He pushed on the door and peered through the shower door at an empty shower.

"What the hell?"

Tom opened the door, and Milly, her hair pulled up as she washed it, started and glared at him.

"Tommy, you get out of here. I need to finish."

Tom backed away and closed the door.

Mildred came out a few minutes later.

"Getting too old to be doing anything in the shower. We'll fall and hurt ourselves."

"You were in there a while. I got worried."

"Had to shave my legs. It's been a while, and I'd like to have some fun later," she said.

Tom smiled and entered the bathroom. He'd waited to shave until she finished.

He hurried through his shaving routine and slipped on his dress shirt.

Mildred finished all of her things, and they walked to the elevator.

Dennis stood outside it as if he'd been waiting for them.

"Just in time. A few guests have sat already. And boy, don't you two look spiffy."

"We wanted to look nice for dinner. Not very often do we get out for dinner," Mildred said.

"Oh, yes. I'm sure. Well, let's go, shall we?"

He led them onto the elevator and threw the handle. The elevator moved more quickly than Tom remembered. They stepped off, and Dennis led them to the dining room.

"Raul will get you a table," he said.

A man in a white jacket stood behind a podium. He glanced up at them.

"I am Raul. I will take you to your seat." He said.

Tom stared at the man. White jacket. Tufts of grey hair flowed out from the chest, and more overflowed from the jacket's cuffs.

Raul grabbed a couple of menus and led them to a table near a window. They passed two other couples—both older, like themselves.

When Raul pulled the chair out for Mildred, Tom smiled.

"Do you get any younger couples or families at the hotel?" Tom asked.

"Not usually. We cater to a certain age group. It just works better."

Tom wondered what he meant about that last comment but sat down, and Raul handed him and Mildred their menus.

"Our specials tonight are gumbo and a crawfish étouffée."

Tom glanced at the other couples in the room. The one closest nodded to him. The other acted as if he weren't there.

"It's a bit weird, isn't it?" Tom said.

"What is?" Mildred replied, staring at the menu.

"This room, this hotel, that water outside the window," he said and stared across the table at her.

"I don't know what you're talking about."

"This whole place is weird, and you know exactly what I'm talking about. You were in the room too. You watched the bed move. You saw the water come over the window. You—"

"Stop it, stop it, stop it," Mildred said. Her eyes welled with tears as she struggled to regain her composure.

"Mildred, calm down. You're going to have to calm down," Tom said.

"Calm down? This hotel is crazy. Our bed was moving. Ocean waves rubbed against the window of our room, and now that man in the corner appears to be eating his wife," she said.

Tom turned around, and the man who'd ignored them sat next to his wife, a knife in one hand, a fork in the other. He cut little pieces off her arm and slid them into his mouth while she carried on as if nothing were happening.

"What the hell?" Tom said and stood up.

He hurried over to the man. Raul grabbed him by his collar and stopped him.

"That man is eating. You will leave him alone," Raul said.

"But he's eating his—"

"No, you will leave him alone. They've been here for a month. They are our best guests in a long time, and we need them to stay."

"But—"

"You will return to your table. I will be there shortly to take your order."

Tom shrugged off Raul's hands and returned to the table.

Raul smiled when he sat down and approached their table.

"Now, what would you like to eat?" Raul asked.

"Is there nothing you can do about that man?" Tom asked.

"He has the meal he asked for. Tomorrow it may be her turn."

Tom stared past Raul to the table, but the couple was no longer there.

"They're gone," Tom said.

Raul turned around, "I guess they had enough to eat."

Mildred only stared at Raul, "I would like the sea bass."

Tom stared at her, wondering how she could eat with what she'd witnessed moments before, but a strange hunger came over him, and he asked for the steak, rare, with mashed potatoes and asparagus. The thought of the juices of the bloody steak flowing into the potatoes, turning them pink, made his stomach growl.

"You've never ordered a steak rare in your life," Mildred said.

"Fine, I'd like it blue," he said.

"We don't cook meat blue. It causes too many issues," Raul said.

"Fine, sear it on both sides and bring it out here," Tom said.

Raul smiled, "And what would you like to drink?"

"A Diet Coke," Tom said, and Mildred nodded.

"Wonderful," Raul said and hurried from their table. He cleaned up the table where the man and woman had sat and pulled the tablecloth off. Blood ran off of it to the floor. Tom watched as small creatures scurried about the floor, sopping up the blood with tiny tentacles. The fascination of it floored him.

"What are you looking at?" Mildred asked.

"Those creatures. They're sopping up the blood," he said.

Mildred turned to look at them. "I guess they are."

Tom stared at her and, not wanting another reaction, ignored her obliviousness. Then he wondered if it were obliviousness or just an absence of caring. Either way, he asked if coming to the Hotel Regal was a good idea. Maybe they should have gone somewhere else, like Las Vegas. They could get their old room, the one they stayed in when they met the family in Las Vegas, but it was too late for that.

He decided they'd leave in the morning. The strangeness of the hotel and the weirdness of the happenings within its walls caused his stomach to roil, toss, and turn.

"I guess you are hungry?" Mildred said.

"Huh?" Tom replied.

"I can hear your stomach from this side of the table," she said.

"Don't you think this place is weird?" he asked, waiting for her response.

"Now, Tommy, don't go messing up our vacation."

He knew with those words they'd be staying, but for how long? He'd booked it for four days, but was there any way to get out of it? He'd think about that over dinner.

Their food arrived, and Tom stared at the blood pooled around the potatoes. The look of it made his stomach roil more, but there was something feral about it. A subtle urge lay under the roiling. He had a hunger he'd never felt, and he dove into the steak, cutting large swaths of the barely warm meat and stuffing them into his mouth. He dragged the beef through the potatoes, drenching them in runny blood.

The nearly pink potatoes covered the pieces of steak as he'd drag each one through canyons of potatoes and waterfalls of brown gravy and ended at spears of asparagus, which he'd place at the tip and shove into his mouth.

Mildred watched this with fascination and fear, but how she consumed her food was no better.

The grilled sea bass rested on a layer of rice, but while it was thoroughly cooked, the grey flesh reminded her of how her mother looked when she died. The grey flesh turned her stomach, but as with Tom, the hunger in her, one that she couldn't place and buried deep within, pulled itself out as she pulled grey flesh from the fish, dug through the tiny white rice, and shoveled it into her mouth.

Tom glanced up at her, watching her eat as they stared at one another, not knowing how they ate. Only an insatiable hunger roared through them.

Raul came to the table, stared at the plates covered in blood and gray flesh, and smiled, "I guess you are hungry."

Tom stared at where the large steak had been. Trails of blood ran through the plate, but the steak was gone. The potatoes and asparagus too.

"I don't remember eating it," Tom said.

"It's fine. Your appetites are fine. They will do nicely," Raul said.

"We'd like the check," Tom said and glanced at Mildred across the table. Grey flesh dangled from her mouth. She nodded, and the meat flopped around the side of her mouth.

He motioned for her to notice, and she slurped it up.

"Oh, we've taken care of your meal tonight. It's the least we could do for your anniversary," Raul said.

The man at the other table turned to their table.

"Your anniversary, too?" he asked.

"Yes," Tom said.

"It's ours and that other couple's as well," the man said and returned to eating a plate full of spaghetti. His wife dug into a large cake, but Tom stared at it. Things were moving around the cake. The woman didn't notice and dug one out and crunched down on it.

The man twirled up his spaghetti noodles onto his fork; then Tom stared closely as they wriggled and squirmed, blood dripping into the marinara sauce. They were worms.

Tom stared across at Mildred. She watched as well, then turned to her plate where she'd believed a piece of sea bass should be. Tom stared.

The sea bass lay on top of a wriggling mound of maggots, while the sea bass was not fish but an arm wrapped in a banana leaf.

Tom stared at his plate.

The bones from the steak he'd eaten lay on the potatoes, which were creamy and filled with tiny white pellets that wriggled and twisted. The bone of the steak was not a cow bone but a human forearm.

Mildred stared from him to his arm, which was no longer there. Mildred's wasn't there either.

"Oh my God," she said.

Tom stood up, grabbed Mildred by the hand, and pulled her through the dining room.

"You can't leave. There is still dessert," Raul said.

Tom ran up the stairs to their room, grabbed their things, and tore off.

Dennis, Raul, and Victoria stood at the bottom of the stairs with Mildred.

"You can't leave," Victoria said.

"Want to bet?"

He grabbed Mildred and pulled her towards the doors.

"I can't go with you," she said.

"Wait, what?"

"This is where I'll be. Tell the kids I love them. You saw me in the shower, but first, you didn't. We had to keep it going. We had to please the hotel. It's done. They've sated it, but I can't leave. It took me."

"No, I can't go without you," Tom said.

"Then you must stay," Victoria said.

"What happens if I stay?"

"The same as the others," Victoria said. "You will notice things. You will find things and want to be gone, but you'll never find a way out. It will sometimes drive you mad, but you will return every day as if you had just arrived. That's what happens to the others." Victoria said.

"Do they know?" Tom said.

"No, and you won't either," Victoria said.

"You will go about this every day. Find out that you've arrived at this place and all it has. You will continue to live this day, every day, and while you descend into madness, the hotel will feed on your fears, on your desires." Raul said.

"You can stay, but you will only know what happened to both of you at this point. The Hotel Regal will keep you."

Tom stared at Mildred, tears in her eyes, and he nodded then thought for a moment.

"This isn't the first time, is it?"

They smiled at him.

In Headlights

Eric John Anderson

"There's something in the road."

I looked up from the hypnotic hold of my phone to see a smattering of strange objects blocking our way.

"What should I do?" Stacey's voice was getting higher, which meant she was starting to panic.

"Slow down. Slow down." I tried to keep my voice calm, even. We had been through enough tonight, and we didn't need another surprise.

My first thought was that an old towel had fallen out of someone's truck, bunched up in a lump and battered by the incessant wheels trampling over and over it. Long dinged by dust and tires.

I was navigating. Stacey said it was because I was the man in the car. I told her that was sexist. The truth was, I had no clue where we were. We had left in such a hurry, I didn't really have time to think of *where* it was we should be running to, just that we should be running *away*.

As Stacey slowed the car, several other objects came into view. Metallic. Odd. Like a couple of bumpers from a car that had been twisted and stretched out in a wreck. Several pieces of charred plastic or carbon fiber were littering the entire two-lane blacktop. It looked as if a large EV truck had fallen apart on the road in a jumbled mass of scorched recklessness.

Maureen began to stir in the back. She had been out cold since we passed the last few streetlights of civilization, her long dark hair falling haphazardly, covering her face. We had only been driving for a few hours or so, fleeing in such a hurry that we didn't have time to think how long this route was going to take. "Where are we?" The sudden deceleration shook her out of sleep, suddenly aware, confusion washing over her languid face.

"Some highway. We probably have about an hour to go." I wasn't about to accelerate the panic already coming from Stacey. The ultra-calm demeanor was a gift and curse from my mother. I took her red hair and femininity. My father dumped me with his anxiety and people-pleasing attitude. The masculine part of him somehow missed me and was injected into his younger son, my brother—the reason I had plucked Maureen out of work this morning and piled her into Stacey's yellow junker car with a suitcase. He was the reason I hadn't planned any of this. After he hits her one more time, you pack up her things and get her out of the house.

The car came to a stop a few yards from the debris. We stared at the carnage in silence. Stacey finally lifted her tight grip from the steering wheel.

"Well?"

"Well, what?"

"What do we do?"

Maureen leaned forward into the gap between our seats. "Can we go around?" she said, as I had the same thought.

I looked over to the shoulder of the highway. On my side was a large ditch, sloping down for several feet. On Stacey's side was a gigantic thicket of sagebrush. We might have been able to push through it, but from where I was sitting, it didn't seem possible.

I knew what Maureen might have been thinking. That age-old urban legend of a woman driving alone at night when she sees some two-by-fours in the middle of the road. She gets out to inspect them and realizes that they have nails sticking out. When she goes to move them out of the road, some guys jump out of the shadows and take her car. Or worse.

My brother really loved that story at summer camp. He would relish in the dark details of a defenseless woman being taken advantage of. For some reason, I imagined him popping out of the shadows in front of us, a cruel grin inviting us back to suffer the consequences of leaving.

"Go around where?!" The panic was definitely taking hold of Stacey now, her little blonde pixie cut falling down in front of her blue eyes, wet with tears forming on the edges. She had gone along with our plan because we were friends in need, but she hadn't known the extent of where we were going. I felt a bit guilty in not at least letting her know the insane route I was taking us through.

Setting down my phone and brushing some cheese dust off my thighs, I unbuckled.

"What are you doing?" Stacey held out her arm and pushed me back into the seat.

"I'm just going to take a look."

"Don't. Matthew, please." Maureen pleaded.

I looked into her eyes. They were entreating me the same way they did this morning when I made the decision to flee. She put her hand on my shoulder. "Let's just turn around." *The woman with the spiked boards.*

"It'll be two seconds. I'll be careful."

My false confidence wasn't so much that I felt brave. It was mostly because I was terrified. We were out here in the middle of the night, and nothing man-made could be seen for miles, aside from this small desert highway.

Stepping out into the crisp August air, I cursed myself for not downloading or printing a map earlier. I stood outside the car for a few moments, trying to listen for any sounds. A slight breeze rustled over the sagebrush. A few crickets chirped out into the night.

I nearly jumped out of my skin as Stacey screeched from inside, "Close the fucking door!"

The door closed a bit more forcefully than I had intended, but I gave her the middle finger in response anyway.

My steps turned into a shuffle as I approached whatever was on the road. The lump of towel seemed to transform color as I got closer. The headlights had washed out and distorted its shape.

It looked animal. About the size of a husky dog. Its legs were long and skinny, piled up in a bunch like it had rolled pretty violently along the asphalt and stopped. I didn't see a head at first, but once I was a few feet away, there it was—large and oblong, lying lifeless on the road.

It was no dog. If it was an animal, it wasn't any I had ever seen. It looked very human, or like it could have been human at some point. What I thought was a dirty towel was some type of clothing. It was scorched similarly to the plastic pieces along the road. I froze. I didn't want to confirm what it was I was looking at.

Bending down, I grasped the closest piece of twisted metal bar I could. I started to push it out of the road, the metal scraping along the asphalt with a high-pitched shrill. As I gripped, the metal became pliable, my fingers sinking into it like bread dough. I dropped it, startled. Looking closer, what seemed metallic silver was actually shimmering as a multi-faceted diamond. This... whatever it was, was defying every physical aspect of metal I had come to understand in my short life.

A sheering *honk* broke me out of my trance. I turned to the car, planning to flip off both of them this time. Instead, I froze.

Silhouetted against the brilliant bright of the headlights was another one of the creatures. Its features were darkened in shadow, but I could sense it was staring at me. A glint of the light was shimmering on two large glass orbs on the front of its face. They looked like disconnected lenses of a pair of sunglasses; they could have been some kind of goggles. It was wearing a similar gray cloth as the one lying on the road, but without scorch marks.

Slowly, I rose from the ground. I was nearly twice its size, a fact that gave me small comfort as my heart was thumping a menacing beat, throbbing up to my head.

I moved my hands and flapped my arms, like someone shooing at a cow in the road, "Go away!"

It didn't move.

With a slow and steady shuffle, I edged toward the side of the road, figuring I could try and get in the car and we would just turn around. I took one longer step. The creature pulled out a small black box from a pocket and pointed it at me. The message received, I stopped. A pit formed in my throat, the fear of unknown violence. What if the thing acted like everyone on Earth and shot first, asked questions later?

Whatever it wanted, it wasn't going to let me get in the car. The option that kept flashing in my mind was to make a break for it— try and outrun whatever went off if it shot the thing pointing at me.

My right foot pivoted, tendons pulled, I was ready to launch.

The creature raised the black box, and I was immediately caught in some sort of force. My body went stiff. It felt like when you sit on the toilet too long and a numbness flows down your calves making it difficult to move. The numbness moved down my entire spine and limbs. My fingers and toes clenched and stuck in place. My hair follicles were burning, my skin tingled throughout with electricity. Body tensing, ripping, reeling. The only desire was to scratch off my skin, peel it away, and rub it sore. I couldn't move any muscles, not even my lips or eyelids. The LED fog lights on the car seeped and burned into my retinas. God, how I wished I could just blink and relieve the pain of those unnecessarily bright lights from burning into my corneas.

Something moved from behind the car. Maureen had exited and was running towards me. The creature turned the black box, freezing her in mid-run, both of our bodies stuck as if lodged in gelatin.

The creature took a few steps towards Maureen and out of the light, giving me a greater look. Its head was oblong, eyes shimmering black glass. Mouth small and flat. I couldn't tell if there was any nose or ears. The skin was cracked and gray, as if leather were left in the desert sun for a few weeks. It was proportionally lanky, the torso being high on spindly legs, its arm dropping lazily down to its knees.

A sudden flash of light behind caught my attention. Stacey was launching herself toward the creature in full swing, an object in her outstretched hand. Possibly the windshield scraper. I couldn't see it properly.

The creature nonchalantly turned and pointed the device at her. The inertia of her swing should have brought her tumbling forward, but the device froze her just as us, only floating in midair.

With the threat of all three of us neutralized, it casually put the device back in its pocket (or what seemed to me a pocket) and strolled over to the open driver's side door.

My vantage point was obscured; I couldn't tell what it was doing. There was some clunking and prying of plastic. The horn honked. If I could have moved, I would have jumped at being startled.

Every now and then, I would see its head pop up over the dashboard. It was throwing pieces of the car and whatever was loose to the ground. I saw my cell phone fly through the air and land in the brush. Whatever it was looking for, it was getting more and more flustered that it wasn't finding it.

The hood popped. It walked around the car, and after some investigation, it was able to find the latch and open up to the engine. It continued searching, pulling out pieces, wires, and tubes. The only means of our escape was being slowly incapacitated, and we were completely useless in stopping the carnage.

It yanked at something and staggered back a bit from the force. From its pocket, the creature produced another small object, this one shiny metal like the twisted bars on the road. It pointed the new device at the car part. After a few beeps, the creature tossed the car part and kept pulling at the engine.

Pointing the device at another part, it made a different set of beeps. The creature flipped the device and used a different trigger. Whatever it was doing was making the car part glow hot red, the creature holding it with no discomfort of burning heat. The part transformed in its hand into a long cylinder rod. Once it finished glowing, the creature put the scanner device back in its pocket and walked towards me.

As it passed, those big black marble eyes turned and bored straight into my helplessly open eyes. A sensation came over me, not like a voice, but more of a feeling entered my head: *Stay calm.*

My throat curdled around a scream that I couldn't manage to release. The creature left the road and rustled through the brush off into the dark desert.

We were left in our statued state. My mind wandered to the events that led to this moment. Maybe we had watched too many shows and read too many memes about abuse. Maybe we were over-reacting.

Nah, fuck that. That was the voice of abusers and so-called family telling us it was our own fault. My brother was never going to stop. No one believed Maureen but me. We were helpless to change anyone, so we were going to take ourselves out of the equation.

I watched Maureen and Stacey, wondering what they were thinking. How we could possibly recover from this. How we would explain it. If we would even try to explain it, or would we bury it deep like everything else. Would we go back?

I was the one who suggested we go through the desert so he couldn't track us. I had gotten us into this situation. It was all my fault.

After what seemed an hour, a high-pitched whir like a broken ceiling fan started up several yards in the direction the creature had gone. A brilliant blue light flooded the entire area. It felt as if we were standing under the noonday sun. This gave me a really good look at our surroundings. Maureen and Stacey were still frozen, their faces in a similar distorted panic to what I was feeling. I tried calling out to them, but the only sound was a gurgle in my throat. A similar whimper came from one of them, possibly Maureen.

The scene of the car looked like we had been in a wreck. Thousands of pieces were littering the road and sand.

The other wreckage on the road near the first creature was in similar disarray. I could see a trail of char and debris leading to where the lights were glowing off in the distance. It was their own vehicle that crashed. The thing must have been scavenging Stacey's old beater for parts to fix his... ship?

Stacey started to move. At first, I thought she had become unstuck, then I realized she was still frozen. Her body was being lifted up by some invisible force. It looked as if gravity had been reversed for only her. None of the many car parts on the ground beside her moved. A few feet in the air, she was instantly out of sight. It was as if a vacuum had been flipped on.

Next was Maureen. The same slow lift until instantly sucked up. I tried to cry. No tears would form. I knew I was next.

A gripping sensation yanked at my gut, an upswing force like a dip in a roller coaster, then I was floating.

Right before getting sucked up, I saw in the corner of my eye the first creature lying peacefully on the road, passed out (or dead.) It began to float up as well, along with all the debris and bent metal bars.

The last thing I remember was the light—so bright and blinding. I still couldn't blink or close my eyes. Nothing but light everywhere.

The burnt red-orange glow filled my eyelids, solar heat warming my skin, sweat forming on my pores. I lifted my arm to block the light as I slowly opened my eyes.

We were on the side of the road. Maureen was lifting her head; Stacey was still out cold. I sat up and looked at our surroundings. In the washed-out sunlight the desert looked so arbitrary, not the sight of incredible horror we felt during the night. I looked over at Stacey's car. A large man wearing a faded blue jumpsuit was standing in front of the engine, inspecting the damage.

"Hello?"

Maureen started to sit up. I put my hand out to stop her, placing a finger to my lips. Stacey started to stir on the other side.

"Hello?!"

Stacey sat up now. Unsure where she was waking up.

"What's going on..."

I shushed her.

Stacey looked at me with eyes that were practically rolling. She replied, despite my waving hands, "Hello?"

The man's footsteps came closer to us.

"What in the hell is going on here?"

No use in hiding anymore, we all slowly got up and brushed the dirt from ourselves. We looked up. The man was in his fifties or sixties, tanned from laboring out in the sun most of his life. The patch on his jumpsuit read *Bob*. His work truck was cracked white paint and rust covered in toolboxes and equipment.

His voice came out gruff and short. "Your shit is blocking the road."

I was about to reply the first thing that came to my head, a lie about why we were there and what had happened. Something about us being ditsy city girls and a gay guy who doesn't know anything about cars. Why was my first instinct to lie?

Before I could get out anything, Stacey spoke up, "We were having some car trouble."

Maureen looked at her in shock. "No, there was this thing..."

"We didn't know what to do, so we thought we would try and fix it ourselves." I cut her off then gave her a look to play along.

"By stripping the whole damn thing?" Bob turned and gave another look at the carnage. He looked at us in disbelief, trying to take in all the information, "Do you have anyone you can call?"

I nodded my head and walked back up to the road. Looking at the car, bits and pieces strewn all over the road, it hit me with the enormity of what had happened last night. The creatures and debris were gone. I wasn't entirely sure if any of it had been real, but then why was our car in pieces? I was sure Bob was thinking we had come out to the desert to take mushrooms and we ended up tripping too hard. He stared at us as if we were completely out of our minds.

Stacey came up to me and spoke under her breath. "What happened to the stuff that was in the road?" She didn't see all of it getting sucked up when we disappeared into the light. At least it wasn't all in my own head.

All I wanted to do was just sit and cry, but it felt like Bob wouldn't appreciate any of that nonsense.

The scorching dry air scratched at my throat. I swallowed what moisture was left in my mouth and wished for a drink of water. Maureen and Stacey joined me as I started searching through the car, the damage more visible. The entire dashboard panel was ripped off and pieces covered the front and back seats. We moved a couple pieces, then I remembered—the creature had tossed my phone out.

Heading to the other side of the road—Bob staring at me in utter confusion—I scanned the dirt and brush until I spotted the bright pink phone cover. Picking it up, I was relieved to see that it was intact, no major cracks or issues.

My face unlocked the phone. It had twelve percent battery left. One bar of service. I stared at the home page, unable to think.

Who could I call? What would I say?

Next of Kin

Adrian Speth

D ouglas insisted on making the drive at night. "Emptier roads,"
he said around his lazy, lopsided grin.

"Who makes a road trip at night?" Grace asked.

"Why waste the daylight on him?"

Grace agreed with cold hands. The trip was for her father, or rather
theirs together, although Grace so rarely saw Douglas anymore that
she often considered herself an only child. They had more or less
parted ways after high school; she had moved to Salt Lake for college
and he'd stayed behind in the red rock, haunting the area they grew up
in. If Douglas was anything, he was haunted, and in turn he haunted
others, haunted Grace.

He had showed up at her apartment without much warning. The
last time she'd seen him was at their mother's funeral a year prior.

"Heard some news," he said by way of greeting. Straight to his
point, no sense of the time or distance between them. He was funny
that way, a side effect of a long-ago summer. "Dad's out of prison."

Grace stood still in her living room. The ceiling fan squeaked above
her. When her vision went fuzzy and her feet threatened to leave the
ground, she focused her eyes on one blade and watched it rotate five,

ten, fifteen times. When she finally looked back at her brother, she was dizzy, but the world was still.

"No one told me," she said.

"I'm telling you."

"Someone else should have said something."

"Did you want to be told?"

She ground the heels of her hands into her eyes. The stars that burst behind her eyelids were bloody. "I thought it would take longer."

"Couldn't stay in Gunnison forever." Douglas shrugged and tilted his head the way he did when he was about to make a joke only he found funny. "Maybe he got out on good behavior."

"It doesn't work like that. And as next of kin, someone should have *notified*—"

"Well, you can ask him why they didn't when we pay him a visit."

She blinked. "You want to see him?"

"Don't you?"

The answer wouldn't come.

Douglas shrugged again. "He's still around. I want to show him that I am, too."

And then there they were, in Grace's beat-up Chevy, the Wasatch lights long vanished behind them. Douglas couldn't drive, another ghost of the summer they turned eleven, but his presence kept Grace awake. He had their father's address, too, though he never said how. She didn't ask. Asking one question might lead to too many others, might give her just enough time to actually think about what they were doing. Five hours southeast to Blanding. It would be a beautiful drive with the sun at either horizon. Instead, it passed by unseen. She hadn't been on the road with Douglas in years, which might have given her another positive to focus on, but as both Douglas and the radio faded in and out with the miles, Grace stopped trying to engage either. The desert sprawled out around them, their wheels kicking up dust.

"Still no husband?" Douglas asked. Grace jumped. He and the radio had been silent for twenty minutes. She shook her head, and he chuckled. "Better hurry it along."

"No, thank you."

"Marriage might settle you down."

"I'm settled." If there was one thing she didn't want to discuss with Douglas, it was men.

He needled. "Something about you, maybe, that scares them all away—"

"Maybe it's you."

His laughter bounced around the cab. "I am prettier."

"We're twins."

"I got a better face."

"Yeah, and look what Dad did to it."

The statement suffocated his laughter. The temperature in the cab dropped. Douglas turned his head and stared out the window. Grace glanced over and then flicked her eyes back to the road. Her stomach churned. For all their childhood fights, and even for this distance between them the past few years, they had been born fifteen minutes apart. First Grace, then him. Nothing separated them. She led, and he followed, and that was how it had always been. She hated when he told her what to do. She hated having to look at the back of his head.

"I'm sorry," she said. When he didn't respond, she reached across the center console and nudged him. "Douglas, come on. Did you hear me?"

"Yeah."

She tightened her grip on the steering wheel, reality creeping in at the edges of her bug-splattered windshield. "We should turn around."

"Why?"

"Or just keep driving." Her words had a pleading edge to them, too sweet for her liking, but she let them come. "We used to make trips like this as kids. We can drive down to Monument Valley or over to Colorado. Find a cheap diner, a cheap motel. What do you think?"

"I think you haven't looked in the rearview mirror once since you got in the car."

"What is that supposed to mean?"

"You don't want to turn around." He kicked his feet up onto the dashboard. "We're going. He's going to see me."

Grace's mind slid. It had happened in the house she learned to walk in, even her earliest memories marred by future events. She remembered the squeak of the front door and the brilliant blood-orange skies during summer heatwaves. She and Douglas rolled around in dust and dry grass as her father knocked around the house with a hammer. Odd jobs he said, as they split eggs onto a sidewalk too hot to touch—

"You're thinking about it," Douglas said.

She bit down on the past. "Am not."

"Then what?"

She couldn't deny him, not with her skull buzzing like this. "We wanted to fry an egg on the sidewalk."

"That heat must have been some sort of record."

"It was hotter the year after."

"Don't hide it away." His voice was easy again, almost gentle now that he was getting what he wanted. "You want this as much as I do."

A shudder crept up her shoulders. "It's my fault, anyway. I took the carton out of the fridge. I knew he was in a bad mood, and I swore we wouldn't get in trouble, especially once he saw how cool it was. You should be blaming me for what happened."

"You already do that. And you already see me." He took his feet off the dash. "It's his turn, now."

She took her foot off the gas and rested it against the brake. Reality blurred again with the yellow lines on the road. Her father's roar reached her before his hands did, and then her frantic scramble out of harm's way that skinned both her knees, and that hammer's silver arc against the sky. Her throat raw around the shrillness of her voice, shouting, "Mama come quick, it's Douglas. Daddy hurt Douglas—"

She hit the accelerator. The truck jerked and sped on towards Blanding.

The house was off the highway, outside the city limits. Grace almost missed the turn. Douglas grabbed her shoulder, jolting her out of the nervous mess her mind had become. "There."

She slammed on the brakes and slid into the turn, forcing them off the blacktop and onto the narrow dirt road. Clouds of dust billowed up around them. Douglas laughed as they shuddered to a slow crawl.

"Careful," he said. "It's lonely, dying out here."

Grace stopped the truck halfway down the road to the house. It was small, its windows curtained against the coming dawn. A screen door hung lopsided up on the stoop. She didn't see a mailbox. They must have just avoided hitting it back when they made the turn.

"Lonelier out here than in town," she said.

"Probably smart," Douglas said. "Who knows what people might do if he tried anywhere closer."

She couldn't take her hands off the wheel. It wasn't too late. She could turn them around right now, speed back to safety. Douglas would be angry, might never speak to her again, but maybe that was for the best. It might settle her the way he wanted, for the two of them and their father to be over and away from each other for good.

"Grace."

She looked over at him. He met her gaze. Hungry eyes. Haunted face. She looked back at the house. "Let's just sit a minute."

"A minute." He settled back in his seat. The desert was pink around them. The sun would be up soon. Something about this would be beautiful.

"What if I can't look at him?" she whispered.

"No one asked you to." Douglas watched the house. "Think he'll really see me? Mom finally did. Just before she went."

Grace's throat was sandpaper. "She missed you."

"You didn't."

"You never left."

"Minute's up."

The door clicked open under his hand. He slid out of the truck and turned away from her, towards the house. The ragged hole in his skull grinned back at her, white bone gleaming under matted black hair and dried blood. She turned away and for the first time looked into the back seat. The hammer lying across the cracked leather felt different somehow, so many miles away from where she'd tossed it inside. Like when she next gripped it, it would rest easier in her hands. Like it might feel almost natural cracking against her father's skull. She took her hands off the steering wheel.

They stood next to the truck in silence. A breeze ruffled Grace's hair, already warm with the promise of the day. The house was still dark, their father likely still asleep. Did he dream about that day the way Grace still did?

"You have to do it," Douglas said. "But I'll go first, if it makes it easier."

When she didn't answer, he tucked his hands into his pockets and started up the road. Grace stared hard at the mess of his skull. In the rosy morning glow, blood shifted to dirt, kicked up from playing in the yard. The imperfect split of an eggshell, yolk oozing onto the pavement, marking the spot Douglas collapsed.

"Wait," she said. "Let me."

He grinned, lopsided, and stepped aside. She led, and he followed, and to the east, the sun rose.

Road to Nowhere

J. T. Seate

A lot of wide-open spaces can be found in Utah. The monuments and canyons are breathtaking, but Arnie prefers roads not always found on roadmaps. Places where cell-phone connections are a crapshoot. The roads less taken were those he liked to travel, ones that gave him time to clear his head. Sometimes, the only place you can be yourself is when you are alone with no one left to disappoint, free of encumbrances and obligations. Free once more and heading west on the rope of highway across desolation. No boring interstates or tourist haunts for him.

Backroads were the way to go. Amidst a landscape dotted with sage and yucca where the Gila monsters and scorpions play, there were decaying automobiles and a few scattered trailer houses strewn about, the only signs of civilization and the only windbreaks in this lonely place. *True Americana*. Beyond, only a wide horizon where the sky dropped behind a brown world. Ahead, the unwritten pages of his future, blank pages yet to be written.

Only one thing could thwart his pleasure was the rare and unexpected treachery of rain-swept roads creating dangerously slick conditions and diminished visibility. A highway when darkness falls was hypnotic enough without the addition of this unseasonable weather. With only the thump-thump of windshield wipers to keep Arnie company as the sky darkened, he kept his eyes peeled for a place to stop before becoming dangerously drowsy. On the side of the road, he caught sight of a dingy building. It looked like an isolated general store. Not part of a nationwide chain, this place. It appeared as though its best days had been in the 1950s, so decrepit its angular verticality was in some doubt, not to mention its ability to repeal hard rainstorms.

His curiosity and the fact that there might not be another watering hole for miles made the decision to stop an easy one. An unassuming neon sign which had long since lost its sizzle perched above the entrance. Arnie guessed it hadn't worked for years.

Even though no other vehicles grazed outside, an OPEN sign was stuck onto the corner of a window. Some fresh beef jerky and a cup of java-to-go was all he needed. He was used to traveling light, especially with the smothered burrito from another greasy spoon still burning his ass.

His car came to a stop in front of two ancient gas pumps—the kind that had glass tops. They looked like two huge, old-fashioned salt and pepper shakers, or maybe bishops from a giant chess set standing like a pair of sentinels guarding nothing of importance. The solitary place reminded him of a child's drawing in its plainness, with rusty props from a bygone era. The structure and surrounding area had the charm of a Quentin Tarantino movie set, which Arnie found kind of appealing.

As if on cue, the wind and rain picked up when he climbed out and slammed the car door shut. The building's gray boards constituting its outer skin turned ebony in the damp night. Arnie put his keys in his pocket and made a run for the front door, the rain crashing off his shoulders like BB shots. He shielded his face from the swirling wet and wind. He halfway expected a tumbleweed to blow past and thought of *Them*, the '50s sci-fi flick about the giant ants, and smiled. The day was finishing with a perfect blend of lonesomeness, lack of comfort, and nostalgia.

Wondering if the store's interior would be equally antique to its exterior, Arnie yanked open a rickety screen door and walked in. The place smelled like coffee grounds and re-circulated cigarette smoke. It had a food counter with four swivel stools. A handful of patrons were scattered around the room sitting with heads bowed over drinks. Some of them had stopped talking to look at him. It was an authentic, old-fashioned, cracker-barrel joint all right—a place that might have been stylish during World War II when people gathered around a Zenith radio and listened to comedy shows and war reports.

Avoiding eye contact with anyone, he strolled to the counter. A plain woman appeared. She stood quietly behind the counter and waited without actually offering service. Even though he wanted to get back on the road, this old place deserved a few moments of observation. The woman tentatively waited for the stranger to make a request.

Arnie slid onto the first stool. "Cuppa coffee, please. Black."

The woman, who didn't look much like a waitress, moved down the counter, picked up a spotted ceramic cup from a plastic tray, and poured a steaming cup of coffee. She wore thick, coke-bottle glasses and a dusty off-white dress. She also looked tired and charmless. Arnie figured charm didn't carry you far in out-of-the-way places such as this.

She set the cup on the counter and studied him through her thick lenses. "Anything else?"

"Not at the moment," Arnie said, and she turned away.

He stared into the cup's black abyss, studying the imaginary tealeaves while the liquid cooled. There was something besides wet streets that gave him pause: the fear of justice. It started as a child when he had stolen a kid's lunch money and got away with it. His slate hadn't been exactly clean over the years since, one of the reasons he enjoyed taking to the road. He had never had to pay for his indiscretions, hoped he never would. Could a cuppa joe reveal his future?

While pondering steam, he absentmindedly looked over his shoulder at the assemblage of early evening customers. Then, he realized something incredible. It was something they all shared. Each of the six men was missing... a body-part. One man was scanning a newspaper with a hand that was minus two fingers. Another lifted his beverage to his mouth with his left arm, the only arm he had. A third man tapped his cane against the wood planks of the floor. His arms, hands, and fingers were all intact, but one of his feet was gone.

There were three more. They were all minus something as well. One, an ear, another, a hand, and yet another, most of his nose. Arnie wondered if he'd happened into some kind of unorthodox convalescence center for war vets.

He took a bolstering sip of his coffee—black and bitter. He waited for the woman behind the counter to saunter in his direction again, and when she did, he said, "I can't help but notice that all your customers have had a bad time. I mean physically."

She frowned. "They've all broken the law, one way or another. Best you don't ask too many questions. Best you drink your coffee and go, Mister."

"Broken the law?" Arnie asked. His curiosity was piqued too much to leave straightaway. "At least tell me enough to keep me awake on the long, lonely drive I've got ahead of me. What's your name?"

"You don't want to know. I don't want to know yours either."

"The name's Harold Springs," he said anyway. "But you can call me Arnie."

"Harold Springs," a man at one of the tables, the one missing a foot, repeated slowly, as if sampling the feel of the words against his lips.

Arnie studied the man for a moment. He snuck second glances at all the men. In addition to the absence of some body part, they had weariness in common. They kept their eyes focused on their tables, apparently having nothing better to do than eavesdrop.

Then, another one spoke. "Go on and tell him your name, Lucy."

"Sam won't like it," she replied.

"Go ahead, Lucy. He wants to know your name," another prompted.

"My name's Lucy," the woman said to Arnie.

He smiled. "Yeah, I figured that out."

One of the men snickered.

Arnie continued. "It's some interesting place you got here, Lucy."

"It's not my place. I mean, I don't own it."

Arnie leaned over the counter, closer to Lucy, and spoke in a hushed tone, taking in more of her features. Her hair was ratted up and brushed back like a born-again, fading country-western singer. Her face reflected any number of hard knocks, most notably highlighted by a crescent scar on her forehead. "So, what's the story on your customers?"

"You have a strong stomach?"

"Cast iron."

"There's a trooper who covers this stretch of highway. He don't cotton to them that cause trouble. Neither does Sam."

"Who's Sam?"

"Sam? He's the one who owns the place."

Arnie was getting nowhere fast. He thought about drinking up and hitting the road. But he sensed a good story here, one he could tell amongst friends someday and title it, *Arnie's Episode of Believe It or Not*. "So, the patrolman and Sam don't like trouble. What has that got to do with these crippled guys?"

Lucy looked horrified. "Don't call nobody that. Don't say... *that* word."

"Sorry. I wasn't thinking politically correct." He thought of the movie again and wondered if there had been nuclear tests in the area way back when. Maybe these unfortunates had been guinea pigs of some sort, but knew he was letting his imagination get the better of him.

Arnie had already stayed longer than he'd intended, but he hadn't realized how long until a car's headlight beams shown through the rain against the dingy plate-glass window like two large cat's eyes. As quickly as the lamps winked out, Lucy skedaddled to another part of the counter with the mystery of the people in the general store left untold.

Lucy, you got some 'splainin' to do, Arnie mused. He heard the door slam shut on the vehicle. Soon, the store's door opened. A tall, strongly built man who looked impressive in a clear rain slicker over his trooper uniform stood inside the doorway. He surveyed the room with the imperious disdain of a sultan observing his minions in accusatory silence.

Then, he looked in Arnie's direction. "Hey, fella," the man said. "That your vehicle parked outside?"

Arnie could feel the strength of the man's gaze through his mirrored lenses. Arnie nodded that it was indeed his vehicle.

"It's the handicapped parking spot, don'tcha know. You got shit for brains or something?"

A handicapped parking sign in front of this dump? Yeah, right, Arnie thought. He also noticed the patrons in the store tensed noticeably but had nothing to say. He stiffened a bit himself, sensing that a not-very-friendly encounter was likely.

"I didn't realize," he answered in a calm voice. "The rain and all. I'll go move my car."

The trooper looked tough for a moment then allowed his face to crack into the slightest of smiles. "Keep your seat. Damage is done. Law's already been broken. Movin' now ain't gonna change that."

The trooper peeled off his wraparounds and strode lazily across the space from the door to the counter in a few strident, John Wayne-like steps, kind of like an Old West sheriff in the movies who doffs his hat to the ladies then sweeps the town clean of armed saddle-tramps. He planted himself next to Arnie and called to Lucy, "Gimme the usual, darlin'."

Arnie felt an uncommon cloak of intimidation. The trooper pushed his hat back on his head and took hold of the mug Lucy presented.

"Where you headed?" he asked Arnie.

"California," Arnie answered.

"This stretch ain't no Bryce Canyon, but it appeals to a certain type, don't it?" A muscle twitched in the trooper's jaw as he glanced at the patrons sitting around the place like they were something he'd want to scrape off his shoe. "Some of these fools had the same intentions at one time, the coast, but they all stayed here."

Arnie looked at them again. "What do you mean? These men were just passing through, all of them with a handicap... uh... disability, I mean... and they just stayed?"

The trooper did a little better than a slight smile. His stone face cracked on either side of his thin lips. 'Didn't have disabilities when they got here.'

A chill snaked up Arnie's spine and prickled the back of his scalp, a sensation akin to an insect with a lot of legs walking in his hair. He realized he didn't want to hear the end of the story. All Arnie wanted now was to pay for his coffee and get the hell out of Dodge. He stood and fished in his pants pocket for money.

"Keep your money, son. I'll take care of it. In fact, I want to buy you one myself."

"No, really. Thanks, but I need to get going."

The trooper put his big hand on Arnie's shoulder and eased him back onto the stool. "You seem to have forgotten you parked illegally. This place may seem like a crap-hole to you, little buddy, but me and Sam, we take pride in this stretch of the planet. We like to keep things nice and tidy and show that crime doesn't pay."

"I think it's very nice," Arnie said, not sounding sincere even to himself. The crap in this particular hole stunk to high heaven. On top of everything else, his bladder hurt. He'd planned to make a pitstop first but had become distracted by the ambience of the customers and the irrepressible Lucy who still had some *'splainin'* to do.

The trooper's smile evaporated. His face turned grim and cruel. "I take breaking the law personal."

Arnie's heart pounded, and his palms began to sweat. He knew the trooper could probably snap him like a twig in addition to being one mean son-of-a-bitch if he put his mind to it.

"I'm going to tell you what happens when you break the law on my watch, and then you can go."

"Okay," Arnie said nervously.

"Joe over there in the corner." Disdain dripped from his voice as the trooper nodded toward the man with only one hand. "He short-changed the waitress who used to be here. Ole Sam, that's the owner, he gave me a jingle, and Joe got what we like to call Frontier Justice. He was the first."

Arnie was incredulous. There could be no mistaking what the patrolman meant. Surely, this was some kind of joke on passersby. "Why's he still here?" he cautiously asked.

The patrolman seemed to enjoy the chance to embellish his story. "Because Joe and the others know what will happen to them if they try to leave. Me and Sam wouldn't take kindly to that. Yeah, they all broke one law or another. Brody over at the table with George, he used to have a heavy foot. Leastwise when he blew down my stretch of highway, he did. And Lucas yonder, the one missing his fingers. Tried to use the five-finger discount on some of the merchandise. Had to take him down a notch. Know what I'm saying?"

Arnie moved his mouth, but words failed him.

The trooper took a sip from his steamy cup, working up his own head of steam as storyteller extraordinaire. He waved his arm across the room. "This bunch here could tell a few tales of their own when neither Sam nor me are around to hear, I'd wager. Isn't that so, boys?"

The men seemed to sink deeper into their seats.

"You'd get a kick out of what happened to one ole boy. Lighten' Jack, I called him. He breezed in one day like he owned the world. A real booger-snot, that one. Had the *hots* for Clara. She used to work here. She liked *him* too. Moral frailty. That was their mistake. You'd never guess what they parted with?"

Arnie didn't want to guess.

"They're gone but not forgotten. Got a few of their offending parts in glass jars. Sam keeps 'em in his office to remind these other knuckleheads that they're actually lucky."

You gotta be shitting me? Arnie thought. *It all has to be some elaborate joke. Must be.* But he didn't really believe it was a joke. His frightened mind pondered what caused one of the men to lose his nose. This trooper was as twisted as dead tree limbs. *Why wasn't this loony in jail?* But the man's freedom wasn't the issue; not becoming his next victim was. Arnie's choice of stops was rapidly becoming the equivalent of winning the lottery to hell. This wasn't just a general store. This was more like the American Southwest's version of Dr. Frankenstein's laboratory. He had to get out. This wasn't the unwritten script he'd bargained for.

The trooper's eyes cut sideways at Arnie. "What none of these chunk-heads knew was that when ole Sam sees something not right, he just calls yours truly, and I catch 'em down the road apiece. I'd drag in more, but Sam can only afford room and board for so many. All they got to contribute is whatever we can fetch for their vehicles and valuables." He waited for his words to sink in then added, "Once you've been sentenced, this is your detention center, you might say. Want to know my opinion? I think they were all lonely cusses, traveling alone and all. But they're as right as rain, now."

Another shiver teased the hair on Arnie's neck. His mouth was dry with fear. He teetered on the stool for a moment and had the sickening feeling the fear was going to cost him his lunch. The trooper was claiming he and Sam maimed these men for one infraction or another. Not only that, but it sounded like they were held in purgatory to suffer their transgressions indefinitely. But the most chilling thought: *What's the penalty for parking in front of some unreadable handicapped parking sign?* Arnie doubted the sign was even there.

With difficulty, Arnie pushed out a few words. "I'm sorry if I broke some kind of rule, officer. I really didn't see any sign out front when—"

"Lucy here had the same problem as you a while back. Ignored the sign just like you. She was too busy thinking about her own business to mind the courtesy for others. Come over here, girl," the trooper said to her.

Lucy, who had been lying low, approached the counter.

"What's your name, boy?"

"Hen... Arnie."

"Show Arnie here your punishment."

Lucy silently stood before them, her face scrunched up like she might be ready to cry. The patrolman reached over the counter and took off her coke-bottle glasses. Behind their protection rested one normal blue eye and one empty socket.

Arnie put his hand over his mouth and hoped he wouldn't puke.

The patrolman handed Lucy's glasses back to her. "She couldn't see all that good anyway,' he told the room. 'Sorta makes you forget about a few scars here and there, don't it?"

Lucy reached for her glasses and put them back on. She looked at Arnie with what he now knew to be only one good eye. *Too late now, brother*, he could almost sense her feeling. *He's shown you his handiwork, so you better run or hide.*

Arnie had to escape this asylum. "I've got plenty of money in my pocket," he said frantically. "I'll pay my fine, whatever it is, if I can just go."

"Well, Arnie, that handicapped sign *could* take some cleaning up so's it's not so easy to overlook especially during a storm," the trooper said. "Guess you sorta feel like I've been pissing on your head and telling you it was rain." Then he chuckled, his attempt at humor. "Me and my big mouth. I guess I've told you a little too much, shown you more. Things can get a little slow out here in the middle of nowhere. Know what I mean?"

"Uh-huh."

"Tell you what. I'll give you a break. Lucy will warm up your coffee so's you won't get sleepy while you're driving, and we'll forget about the whole thing. Besides, you've probably got people waiting for you out there on the coast."

"Yes, I do."

"Give him his coffee with a little sweetener," the trooper instructed Lucy.

She returned with a fresh pot and refilled Arnie's cup.

"You put in the sweetener?" he asked.

"Yes," she said and disappeared.

"Ain't she a sweetheart? A little sweetener in the java helps to stay alert."

"No, thanks. The caffeine ought to do it."

The trooper's good-natured smile faded again. "The weather is a cocksucker right now. I don't want to have to deal with an accident on my stretch of the highway. Drink up. It'll give you just enough time to hear what George did to get his nose caught in a wringer."

Did he have a choice? Arnie felt weighed down by the sweat on his collar. A wisp of steam off the cup's surface reminded him of how quickly normalcy can evaporate. You go through life thinking you're safe from all the nonsense in the world then, *POW*, you find yourself in a place which reveals the randomness of danger. You find that security is an illusion. No one is really safe from weird shit. These revelations had shattered his fragile hope of hitting the road in one piece, literally.

He hadn't seen a jukebox, but some old country and western song suddenly wafted through the room, adding to the unreality of the situation. His world had gone topsy-turvy. Could it all be a horrible dream, a delayed reaction to the doobie he'd smoked after that spicy burrito? What would happen if Trooper John Wayne searched his car? For sure, this situation wouldn't end like a Cheech and Chong comedy.

Some of the maimed men were looking at Arnie now, their faces revealing no emotion other than resignation. One of them picked up the words in the song, his whiney voice screechy and out of tune.

"Drink up, boy," the trooper said again.

It was all just noise in Arnie's head. The trooper who wallowed in his power over others and to hell with due process wouldn't shut up. The warbling singer sounded like a sick puppy. And there was an incessant buzzing in Arnie's ears that sounded like a nest of stirred-up hornets. Would this psychopath cop really let him go? He looked into the coffee cup and wished it held the secrets of the universe, or at least a way out of this mess. He never took sweetener. They could be little packs of poison. Maybe he could throw the coffee into the face of this self-righteous judge and juror and make a run for it? That might be the ticket. One sip and he would decide.

Light shined through the dirty plate-glass window. *Headlights. Another vehicle.* Hope zipped through Arnie like he'd touched a live electrical wire. Someone else coming in. Maybe this would break the spell. Maybe this would change the equation. Alter the series of events.

The trooper was still facing Arnie, seemingly uninterested in another arrival. Arnie didn't turn to look either. He just looked into Lucy's coke-bottle glasses that covered her goo-goo-googly eye. He heard the door open and slap shut.

"Hey, Sam, got us another one," the trooper shouted at a huskily built man who'd just entered the store.

The coffee-throwing idea disintegrated. The place carried the fetid smell of sweat and fear—both belonging to Arnie. His body provided the humidity the air lacked. He was sweaty all over now, even in his crotch. He pathetically wondered if he'd suffered the indignity of wetting himself. At this moment, he would have been happy to take on encumbrances and obligations from his past.

His mouth already tasting of strong caffeine and cotton, Arnie took the cup in his trembling hands and drank before he was once again ordered to do so. He winced as the coffee was bitter and far too hot. His face tingled. Then it did more than tingle. It started to ache. Sharp pain followed. Unbearable pain. Was this the justice he'd always feared?

Trying to convince himself nothing was amiss, that there was still a way out, that everything was still right with the world, Arnie set the coffee cup on the counter after his first sip of the hot brew only to see his lips still clenching tightly to the cup's edge.

His hands flew to his mouth and touched his exposed teeth and the ragged edges of burned flesh. He saw his reflection in a mirror behind the counter. His face looked a bit like a laughing skull. He tried to form a word, but his jaw flapped uselessly.

"Your main crime is you're the kind that talks too much, kinda like me, but not now," the trooper said and then guffawed.

No California. No happy trails, partner.

"Sometimes you just have to laugh at the way things turn out and pay the price. Looks like you'll be laughing permanent-like," the general store's owner, now standing next to Arnie, offered as Arnie started to scream.

The Bear River Wellness Institute

James Fritz

M onday, November 7

At 3:27 AM, two men broke into my bedroom and forced me up. Ten minutes to pack. No breakfast, no time to say goodbye to Mom and Dad. In Utah, it's legal if your parents sign off on it. It's called a parental escort service. I call it legal kidnapping.

I'm not going back to school. Instead, they enrolled me at the Bear River Wellness Institute. Took five hours to get here. There's nothing around except trees.

Did they get sick of all the pranks at school? Nobody proved that I masterminded the Unscrewing. Besides, that was our senior prank. Everybody bore responsibility for that. But I'll be the first to admit that listing the principal's house on Realtor.com was my idea... and the cow prank was, too.

Okay, I'm guilty of a lot. But I don't deserve *this*. I don't take drugs or sleep around or get drunk. I just play pranks.

Upon arrival, me and the other newbies had a seminar with Ms. Hardley, the headmistress. She's half parrot, half human. She screeched for an hour and fifteen minutes. Our parents are sick of us, kids are out of control today, we won't leave till we submit to the Program, blah-blah-blah.

After the invocation, a dorm parent helped me unpack. She said that the school grounds used to be a hostel. A more fitting title would be a hostile. My room's got a bed with the thinnest mattress on Earth, a dresser that's missing a drawer, and a squeaky chair with a desk. There's asbestos in the ceiling. A single light bulb hangs over the room. But the absolute worst part is the posters in the hallways. *Work Equals Freedom. Submission is the key to redemption.* They should make one that says, "*Leave the past in the past: your parents did.*"

Friday, November 11

Got through my first week at Bear River. I still haven't memorized all the rules. They gave me an entire packet. Here are some of the good ones:

1. No eye contact with students

2. No makeup

3. No shaving

4. No talking

5. No touching anyone

6. Leave stall door open

7. Keep hair in braid

Yeah... they don't have rules like that in prison. Compared to this, Utah Correctional is a five-star hotel. When you're an adult, you have rights. If you're a minor, your parents can take them away with a pen stroke. But if they think they can take the joker out of me, I'll be here until I turn eighteen.

But at least I'll have Anan to hang with. I met him during kitchen duty. We talk whenever the dorm parents aren't around. He's a bigger rule breaker than me. His parents shipped him all the way from Florida. Correction: his stepfather did... for sleeping with his mistress. What better way of shutting a kid up than sending him to Bear River?

We've been brainstorming different pranks to pull. It's been months since I've pulled one off. I've got the itch. This place could use some new decor.

Friday, November 18

I woke up at 2:47 AM to hang up the new posters. Anan is quite the artist. Some of them were masterpieces. I wanted to keep the one that read *Submission is the key to orgasm,* but Anan talked me out of it. I hung it right on Hardley's door.

It took two hours for the dorm parents to take them down. We put them everywhere: in the bathrooms, on the doors, in the kitchen, on the ceiling. I don't know how Anan got all the paper and tape. A good prankster never reveals his secrets.

They're going to have a seminar for us tomorrow. Rumor is that when they find the masterminds, they'll send them to the Rehabilitation Station. Anan told me that the RS is Bear River's version of solitary confinement.

I don't care what they do. Listening to Hardley screaming was worth it. The parrot almost had a conniption.

Saturday, November 19

Next time I see my parents, I'll gouge their eyes out. Then I'll make them sit through a seminar.

Hardley's got the process down. First, you wake up all the students in the middle of the night. Then you put them in a room with all the windows covered and no food or water. Once the seminar starts, you're time deprived, sleep deprived, and food deprived.

They played the theme from *2001: A Space Odyssey* when we walked in. We had to lie down on our backs, clap our hands, and scream. For fifteen goddamn hours. They make the students do shit like this during every seminar. Some of the veterans told me that a few months ago, they had all the students smack pool noodles on the ground until their hands bled.

The dorm parents walked around and asked if we had anything to confess. If you were smart, you made something up. I confessed that I made love to a Rottweiler and did 8-balls on the weekends. What's crazy is that they believed me. According to their logic, everybody is guilty of something. If you deny that, you're resisting the Program.

Anan confessed that he got a blow job from Ms. Hardley. Unfortunately, the dorm parents didn't believe that. The guards came in and threw him out. I think they put him in the RS for a breakdown.

Thursday, December 1

Okay, now I'm really fucking worried. Two weeks, and no Anan. Is he still in the RS? Did they expel him or transfer him? Is he still alive? There's a rumor that the school kills some of its students. I wouldn't be surprised if they did, but how could they get away with it? The parents would sue the school into oblivion if that were true. Then the police would come and shut it down.

Hardley would know. She keeps records on everybody. The only problem is that I'd have to break into her office. Guards stand outside 24/7. Can I draw them away somehow?

Fuck... things have gotten so bad without Anan. I forgot to untie my shoelaces before a room inspection and got knocked down a level in the Program. Now they get to treat me like a six-year-old again.

During the latest seminar, they had each of us sit on stage while the rest of the students insulted us. Crack whore, druggie, cow face, pork barrel, scale breaker. Don't get me wrong: I couldn't care less what some rando on the street thinks of me. It's different when the insults come from your friends. The only reason the Program functions is because the students go along with it. As long as you're not getting hurt, who gives a fuck what happens to anybody else?

Hardley called it attack therapy. A nice euphemism for child abuse.

Thursday, December 8

One of Bear River's sister schools shut down. We onboarded 47 new students this week. But get this: one of those 47 is Anan's brother, Derrick. He got sent away for throwing a beer bottle at his stepfather. Doesn't take any shit. He and Anan must have been really close. He asked me to tell him if I hear any news about his brother.

The hostile's completely overcrowded. I've got two roommates now. We alternate sleeping in bed. Hardley implemented food rationing to deal with the extra students. All she cares about is green. The less she has to spend on us, the better.

But there is a silver lining to all this: we've been stretched to the limit. There's a tension in this place that I didn't feel when I moved in. The dorm parents are starting to feel it, too. They've been sending more people to the RS, sometimes for no reason at all.

There's talk of a rebellion brewing. Derrick told me that the tentative date is next Friday. As a professional troublemaker cum trickster cum prankster extraordinaire, I'd be remiss if I didn't do everything I can to help. I've been tasked with pulling the fire alarm. All the exits will automatically unlock. They won't be able to keep us trapped any longer.

We're mad as hell, and we're not gonna take it anymore.

Friday, December 16

Twenty minutes before Armageddon. I'm shaking as I write these words. Everything's ready. Derrick broke into the kitchen and stole all the knives. I've got mine on my desk, and I'm not afraid to use it.

The official plan is to break into the computer lab and destroy all the hardware. Since all of our classes are online, the school won't be able to function without the desktops and monitors. After that, it's every man for himself.

But me and Derrick have a special mission. We're going to find out what really happened to Anan and the other students who disappeared. Once the alarm sounds and the guards are drawn away, we'll break into Hardley's office and go through her files. See what the parrot has been hiding from us.

Five minutes 'til freedom...

Saturday, December 17

I know the truth. The honest, brutal, unvarnished truth.

Bear River was never just a school for troubled teens. It was a place for parents to send their children to have them murdered. All the kids who were sent to the RS were killed and buried somewhere in the forest. My parents never knew about the school's ulterior purpose, but Anan's did. His stepfather paid $385,000 to have him killed.

I've got all the evidence in front of me. Two backpacks full of files from Hardley's office. Checks written from Anan's stepfather. A list of liquidated students. Handwritten letters from parents with their final words to their condemned children. Thankfully, the parrot never made the move to digital.

The riot went off perfectly. It was insanity. Half of the students escaped while the other half stayed and trashed the place. The hostile is beyond repair. All the windows are broken, the electronics are toast, the light bulbs are shattered. Somebody started a fire in the kitchen and burned the fucker down. Good riddance.

Me and Derrick stole some of Hardley's money and checked in at a motel a few miles away. The instant we went to our room, he broke down. Cried for almost thirty minutes. Took a pillow and screamed into it. There was nothing I could say or do to comfort him.

But there is something we can do for Anan. The moment that we get our hands on a laptop and scanner, we're digitizing everything and putting it online. The world has to see what's going on. Bear River was just one school in a network. I won't rest until every one of them is closed.

If he were alive, Anan would do the same.

Animal Avenger

C. H. Lindsay

One prong from a buck's antler
broken off by the trucker
who ignored the sign.

Two unlucky rabbit feet
ripped away from furry host
by one careless swerve.
Three delicate garden snails
baked onto summer asphalt,
wandered from their yard.

Four bruised chicken legs and wings
severed from the breast and back,
for turning around.

Five desiccated serpents
squashed, slithering too slowly
for driver's patience.

Six days after rain begins,

moldering body parts merge,
form a new being.
Seven weeks the monster lives
avenging animals left
scattered on the road.

The Unseen Graveyard

Emily Harney

B eams of the dull headlights faintly illuminated the white lines in the road. *I Will Always Love You* played softly on the radio. A dim green light filled the interior of the car from the dashboard. Sherrie rested her head gently on the cold glass of the passenger-side window. The drone of the highway lulled her into a soft sleep. Her shallow breath left small clouds of fog on the window.

Her head bobbed gently as the car bumped along the deserted stretch of I-80. Streetlights were few and far between, and there had only been a handful of cars passing on the other side of the highway. The inky night sky blurred amongst the deep grey clouds. Light snowflakes began to fall, landing lightly on the windshield.

The sound of the wiper blades slowly rocking back and forth brought a small smile to Sherrie's lips. She recalled being a little girl, sitting in the middle of the bench seat of her dad's truck, plowing through neighborhoods in the winter.

He smoked Marlboro Reds. The sound of the crinkling paper as he held the lighter to the end rang through her head. He would roll the window down just a little so he could ash outside, and the brisk air would bite at her pink cheeks. She loved the smell of cigarette smoke mixed with snow.

Before they'd leave the house, her mother would bundle her up in her warm, winter coat and put on her hat with the long ears and poofy ball and make a bow under her chin. She would kiss Sherrie's cheek softly and tell her to keep an eye out for the reindeer.

A small tear slid down Sherrie's cheek. It had been ages since she'd thought of her parents. They died in a car accident when Sherrie was just ten years old. Some drunk driver, or so she'd been told, had been driving behind them as they headed home from a night out. It seemed that he'd been angry that her parents were driving cautiously in the snowy conditions. He'd been flashing his headlights at them and eventually sped up to go around their car. He clipped the back bumper and sent the car spinning until it slammed headfirst into a tree just off the embankment of the road. Her parents died instantly.

Sherrie had been left at home with her aunt. They'd watched movies and ate pizza and had ice cream for dessert. It was the best night of her life, until the cops showed up, and Sherrie's aunt hit the floor in a puddle of her own tears.

At that thought, Sherrie's eyes jerked open. The smell of cigarette smoke, cold air, and light snow filled her nose. Panic rushed over her. She tried to sit up to get her bearings but found she was unable to move. She reached for the door handle, but she couldn't lift her hand. Her eyes darted around the car frantically, unable to turn her head.

Her heart began to race and sweat beaded at her hairline. The window fogged around her.

"Oh, good," a deep voice echoed beside her. "You're awake."

Terror shivered down Sherrie's spine.

Whose car is this? she thought. Confusion sloshed around her brain, trying to understand the situation she was in. Who is driving? Where are we going?

She tried to speak, but only a faint whisper escaped her mouth. Her breathing became rapid and shallow. More tears streamed down her face.

A large, warm hand landed on her thigh. The skin was rough, calloused. She flinched, though her body didn't move at all. She attempted to scream, but still, nothing came out but a small grunt.

"Don't be like that," the voice commanded. It was a deep voice. Husky and rigid.

Sherrie closed her eyes, willing herself to move, to scream, to do *anything* but sit there, frozen and afraid. She knew it was useless, but she tried anyway.

The rough hand squeezed her thigh. A piercing pain shot up her leg and reverberated deep in her hip. He's strong, she thought. A wave of panic tore through her. She didn't stand a chance of fighting him.

"Nothing to be scared of," said the voice. He released his grip and moved his rough, gnarled fingers further up her thigh. "I won't hurt you."

Every fiber in Sherrie's body was on fire. Her nerves were trembling, and she couldn't contain the tears pouring down her face. They'd made a small puddle on the handle of the old car. She glanced down, only to find that there was no handle. Her eyes darted towards the window, but the lever to roll the window down had been removed. She was trapped. There was no way out.

An hour had passed, and the man next to her kept his hand clenched on her upper thigh. The snow outside had gotten heavier. The thud of the windshield wipers was now loud and clanging, quick and sharp. Not like the sound that Sherrie loved as a child. The road was covered in white. She could no longer watch the lines of the highway blur past her as her head still leaned against the cold window.

She felt a rush of air from the heater. It smelled dusty and warm. A small relief in the nightmare she'd found herself in. The sound of crinkling paper lit up beside her, and the car filled with the smell of cigarette smoke once more. The brisk, winter air rushed toward her as the man rolled down his window just a little. He squeezed her thigh roughly as he took a long, slow drag.

Sherrie shuddered under his touch. She felt her body physically shudder. Some feeling was coming back. A burst of hope flushed through her veins, quickly followed by a wave of nausea as she remembered she couldn't get out of the car, and there was no way she could fight him off. Another tear slid down her cheek.

With a deep breath, she tried turning her head. If she was going to die tonight, she at least wanted to see the bastard that was going to do it. Her head turned slightly, now facing forward to look out of the windshield. The snowflakes rushed toward the car at an alarming speed. They slammed into the windshield, and the wipers quickly swept them away. There had to be at least two feet of snow surrounding them.

"Pretty, isn't it," the voice next to her said. Again, he squeezed her thigh, moving his hand a little higher this time.

Vomit swelled in the back of Sherrie's throat.

Gently, she glanced from right to left, trying to get any sense of where they were. She wasn't sure when she'd gotten into the car or what direction they'd been heading. She hadn't seen an offramp or freeway sign the whole time she'd been awake. They could be anywhere at this point.

The dim headlights shone across a metal guardrail to the right. She glanced to the left, finding a dark figure jutting high into the black mass of night. Sherrie realized they were in a canyon. Her heart dropped. Even if she could get out of the car, where the hell would she go in weather like this?

As his rough hand slid up Sherrie's thigh a little further, the car fishtailed in the snow. He yanked his hand away to grab the wheel. As he turned the car, Sherrie's body flung forward, the seatbelt jerking her back hard against her seat. This time, she landed facing the driver of the car.

Rough, leathery, wrinkled skin covered his hands and face. A long, deep scar ran down the man's face from his hair line, across his nose, through his lips, and down his chin, ending at his collarbone. It was rough and worn. It left his smile crooked. His lips didn't quite line up.

He had purple scars across his hands. His knuckles were more gnarled than they felt on Sherrie's skin. They were swollen, and his fingers were crooked. His nails were yellow and cracked and caked with dirt underneath. He gripped the steering wheel so tightly his knuckles were bone white.

The car righted itself, and he turned to look directly at Sherrie. His eyes were black wells of nothing, deep and frightening. His crooked lips curled over yellowed teeth, stained from years of cigarettes and coffee. He was missing one tooth in the front, and a foul stench emanated from his mouth, wrapping itself around Sherrie like a cloak. Again, she felt the vomit push at the back of her throat.

She stared at him with wide eyes, her body trembling as he leered at her. A small, white clump of saliva had formed in the corner of his mouth. He licked it away with a thick, heavy tongue. Sherrie closed her eyes, willing herself to forget the image.

The snow had begun falling so hard that they were enveloped in a sheet of white. The man pulled the car to a stop on the edge of the road. He turned the flashers on and put the car in park. Sherrie quivered as he leaned toward her and unclicked his seatbelt and then hers. She leaned back towards the door. She finally had some feeling back in her body. But now what? she thought.

"You don't remember, do you?" he asked. He stared at her, almost panting while he watched her tremble.

She stared back, unable to move. This time from fear. Whatever he'd done to her had started to wear off, and she had more movement in her limbs.

"You were so young," he said. "Back then. I remember. Do you?"

Sherrie searched her brain, trying to figure out how this man could possibly know who she was. When I was young, she thought to herself.

The memory hit her like a Mack truck. This man was the one driving the car that fateful night. This man killed her parents.

A deep, guttural scream launched from her throat. She flung her head back, scratching desperately at the door, knowing there was no handle to let her out. She was suffocating in the memory. She couldn't breathe.

The man lunged forward and grabbed her by the back of the head. He pulled her face in close, his rotten breath stinging her eyes. He smiled at her then dragged his thick, dry tongue along her cheek.

"I knew you'd remember," he whispered and then slammed her head hard into the dashboard. It cracked against her skull, and a small trickle of blood ran down the fake leather, pooling at Sherrie's feet.

A deep cold settled itself deep in Sherrie's bones. She rustled at the feeling. She couldn't remember ever feeling this cold. It was as if her bones were made of ice. She twitched. Her hands were numb. They tingled and prickled as she shifted.

Her eyes were heavy and gritty. Her head throbbed, and she could feel something cold and soft gently landing on her skin. She lulled her head from side to side, groggy and uneasy. The taste of dirt and blood filled her mouth. She tried to lick her dry, sore lips but ran her tongue along a rough cloth instead.

With a shudder, Sherrie forced her eyes open. They were swollen, and everything around her was hazy. The gently falling snow slowly came into focus, landing on her eyelashes and the tip of her nose. She shivered.

Her bare legs were buried in snow. She couldn't feel them. No twitch under the snow, no movement at all. The skin of her bare breasts was turning blue as the snow continued to fall around her.

A hollow scream escaped her lungs, muffled by the dirty sock that had been shoved violently in her mouth. She yanked at her hands, trying to free them from the metal guardrail they were roughly tied to. The freezing temperatures had frozen her fingers solid. As she tried to force her arms forward, the index finger of her left hand snapped. Another deep scream shattered the silence of the falling snow.

The spring thaw came early. The mountains sprung to life with lush green in early May. It was our favorite time of year. The earth smelled fresh, and the air was filled with sweet floral scents. We loved driving the canyons, watching the world wake up from its slumber.

We packed our car with a picnic and headed up the canyon towards Coalville. As we headed higher up the canyon, we came around a bend followed by a blind curve. My husband slowed the car, then rolled to a stop.

On the side of the road, tied to the guardrail was the body of a naked woman. She was in perfect condition. The deep, cold winter had preserved her. She had a dirty, bloody sock shoved in her mouth and what appeared to be a severely broken finger. Her eyes were open and frozen in a look of horror.

"What in the actual fuck," I whispered. My body trembled at the sight of her.

"We'll call the police as soon as we pull into Coalville," my husband said, his voice shaking a bit.

We got back in our car, and I noted the milepost we were closest to as we started up the canyon so I could let the cops know where to find the body. As we climbed the canyon further, nearing the summit, a car came up behind us, speeding wildly and flashing its headlights.

"It's early," I said, turning to my husband. "Why is he flashing his lights at us?"

A small wave of fear washed over me. My husband was nervous. I could tell by his bone white knuckles gripping the steering wheel. He rolled down his window and waved the guy around. The man honked and reared up behind us.

With a heavy thud, the stranger slammed into the back of our car. It sent us spinning, and before I knew it, our car had smashed into the guardrail, and we flipped. It felt like we were falling for ages before the car plummeted into the ground below.

All around us stood tall trees and cold earth. The interior of our car was stained with blood and shattered bone shards. Littered around us were the bodies of others, pushed from the road by a man with a taste for blood. Nobody would find us down here.

Just Around the Bend

Danielle Harward

My hands gripped the steering wheel, and my spine snapped straight at the sight of a young man trudging along the side of this cursed road. After you pass the same sign, so many times you stop paying attention, but now, my eyes were wide, coming back into sharp focus.

He was tall, just like the man from all those years ago. I'd barely seen him in the moonlight... *No!* I blinked the nightmare away. *This man was not him.* This man had blue jeans splattered with mud, a coat hugged tightly around him against the cold as if that would protect him from anything. His long legs strode forward with purpose, strong and capable. He sported brown hair slicked back and gelled into place. A sharp jaw, thin lips.

He was a lighthouse in my storm. My God, I was barely able to focus on the road as I drank him in. I glanced in the mirror, eyeing my wrinkled neck and smoothing out my white hair before I shifted the clutch into a lower gear, slowing the momentum of my Thunderbird. The trees loomed above us, angry giants waiting to exact their revenge.

The shadows stretched towards him, curling and twisting their way closer. I swallowed, fighting the anxiety bubbling up my throat as my brakes squeaked. He would think I was crazy. They all did. I couldn't blame them. I sounded crazy. Even when I rehearsed the words to myself alone, I couldn't get them to sound entirely convincing.

I remembered the confusion on each of their faces. A young woman whose brows pulled together as she demanded I stop lying to her. An elderly man my age who slowly fell into a state of shock. And many more failures that haunted me, their faces flashing behind my eyes, their screams permanently etched into my memory. But I had to try. If I did this just right, maybe he wouldn't end up like the rest of them.

"Hey," I called to him as the window lowered.

It came out raspy and desperate. I cursed myself for not clearing my throat first.

The young man eyed me cautiously as he bent down, his brow raised, his mouth set in a slight frown, but upon seeing my car, his hazel eyes lit up, "Woah! You don't see a classic like that around very often." I didn't have to force the smile I flashed him. I loved this car, spent years building it, poured thousands into the custom paint, the red leather interior, and a few engine upgrades that were less than legal.

"Yeah," I said, pride unmistakable. But I needed him to get into my car, and that was a more difficult task. If he didn't, he would die a terrible death. Just like they all had. The memories rushed over me like a wave, and my easy smile became forced. "Need a lift? Nearest town's pretty far away."

The young man debated with himself for a moment, eyeing the road ahead, the dark forest on either side looming above us, the grey clouds in the sky blocking out all possible light and only adding to the cold. I wanted to scream, *get in, get in—GET IN—*but I held the words trapped behind my teeth, clenching them until it hurt. The people I met on the side of the road always hesitated, but I hated being ignored.

Finally, *thankfully,* he gave in. Whether it was my wrinkled skin that convinced him I wasn't a threat, or he simply liked my silver Ford Thunderbird, I didn't care. My shoulders dropped a bit as he pulled open the passenger door and slid into the seat. Before he had fully put his seatbelt on, I got us moving again, slapping down the clutch and shifting up through several gears, letting the car roar like an angry animal beneath us.

I had just passed the sign cheerfully announcing *Heber 30 Miles* as we climbed higher into the Provo canyon. A sign I knew too well. I could count how many power lines we would pass on this godforsaken road and the moment the boulders piled on the left side after the second bend would come into view. I could predict down to the second when a small animal would race across, a squirrel or chipmunk, maybe even a rabbit, though it was too fast to be much more than a blur. Then came a second bend, sharp enough it would make us lean in our seats, and finally the raven angrily cawing at us. All of it seared into my memory.

But maybe if I got him to stay with me, maybe if I got him to *believe* me, things would be different this time.

The young man was relaxed into the seat when I glanced over at him, his eyes roving over the red leather interior. Good. The less he paid attention to the landscape around us, the better. His short brown hair reminded me of the way I'd wore mine at my first office job. But my blowhard boss at the time had forced me to cut it. Thirty years later, when I was the one who sat in the big corner office, I had grown it out again. By that time, it was thin and silver.

"Name's Frank, by the way," I said as I eyed the road ahead of us. I knew I didn't have much time. I needed to tell him what was happening before he realized it. Because whenever they realized it on their own, it was always so much worse. Maybe, if he got to know me first, he might trust the words I needed to share.

The young man leaned back in the seat and rested his arm on the window. "I'm Rodney."

"What brings you out here, Rodney?"

"I was on my way to see my girlfriend up in Heber, but my car broke down a few miles back." He ran a hand through his slicked back hair with a shake of his head.

"Rotten luck," I said as the road made a smooth and gentle turn around the first bend. I could already see the smooth orange and brown sheen of the rocks piled high on the left side of the road coming into view. Once, I tried to turn around, to go back down this god-forsaken mountain road. Instead, I found myself climbing higher and higher all over again.

In front of us, the small creature raced across the road. I used to slam on my brakes for it, but I had passed it enough times to know that even if I did hit the creature, it would be back the next time around.

Rodney chuckled. "It is what it is. Where you headed?"

"Heber as well," I said, hoping the lie didn't sound as obvious to him as it did to me. I swallowed and glanced sideways at him. He seemed entirely engrossed in the radio dials as his fingers brushed over them.

"Oh really? You live there or just visiting?" asked Rodney.

"I lived—live," I corrected myself, "a bit further south, St. George actually." My home lingered in my mind. The blue of my infinity pool and the white of the marble columns always looked brighter right next to the red rock. It made for great pictures at parties, which I held at least three times a month. Large lavish get togethers where I rubbed elbows with some of the city's most elite. Here though, nothing was bright or warm, and the silence was *deafening*.

Rodney nodded, his gaze wondering out the window towards the darkened mountainous forest as he said, "Some great hiking trails down there."

I needed him to stop looking outside. There had been too many times where my passenger noticed the repetition before I could properly explain what was happening to them. Those ones were the worst. They always thought I was the danger, swiping at me and screaming like that would help anything. Rodney seemed interested in cars. Perhaps I could distract him with the history of this one. "In fact," I said, "some of the people who helped me with this car are out there, they left their mark in the stitching." I said, pointing to the wall beside the glove box that had *Omalley's* imprinted on it.

He raised a brow, "I thought Omalley's went out of business a while ago?"

I swallowed hard, my throat suddenly dry. *Out of business?* Could I really have been stuck here long enough that an entire chain of mechanics went out of business? There were no indications to tell me otherwise. No sunrise or sunset to mark the days. The clock in my car didn't even shift more than ten minutes. I clutched at the steering wheel, trying not to show Rodney how much his words made me want cry and rage and howl.

Instead, I forced a shrug, "Might be one of the few left open."

"Huh," Rodney said, more an acknowledgement than an agreement. But at least he was now studying the imprint instead of paying attention to the landscape.

My stomach twisted and threatened to spill any contents remaining within it. Though my wife had left me a few years before I took this ruinous drive through the mountains, part of me wondered, even hoped, she might be concerned for me. Might be looking for me. But the other part of me, the more logical part, knew she was likely glad to never hear from me again. What's more, she would have felt justified in it. She was the only one I told of my blunder on the road. I hadn't been able to hold myself back from telling her with the memory so fresh on my mind. I couldn't un-see the whites of his shocked eyes or the bump followed by crunching and screaming like I'd never heard before. I stammered and stuttered while I told her the story, still in shock.

She'd been disgusted that I never looked back.

But I knew I'd lose every bit of the influence I'd scraped together the past several decades if I had.

The loop started a few years after that. I couldn't truly remember how I had gotten back to this road. The details were foggy. But I found myself driving once more in the very place I had spent years avoiding. I tried to escape it. Even tried to run my car off a cliff to make it stop when I realized I was stuck. But I just woke up behind the wheel, as if I had fallen asleep while driving. It was then I had truly and fully realized there was no escape. The thought invaded my mind like a snake intent on squeezing every drop of hope from my bones, a torturous aching feeling I couldn't escape. I had gasped for air like I was drowning, and by the time I was done slamming my fist into my steering wheel and tearing out my own hair, the loop had reset once more.

Rodney would notice the repetition soon enough too. Which meant I was running out of time. He had to understand what was going on so he could *live*. I was tempted to continue the small talk—to ask about his girlfriend or maybe even if he was going to university—to build more trust between us. But I couldn't linger on these topics too long. The last time my passenger had realized before I told them, she launched herself out of the moving car to escape me. I remember looking in the side mirror as her forearm snapped when she hit the road, bone sprouting from her skin. The white stark against all that red.

No, instead of the small talk, I needed to get a sense of how Rodney saw the world before I presented him with the horrifying facts. At least if I did that, maybe I could find a way to tell him in terms he would understand.

"Tell me, Rodney," I asked, "Do you believe in things that are not of this world?"

His brows scrunched together, "You mean like God?" In his voice, I could hear the petulant annoyance that often comes from youth when the elderly try to teach them. I was like that once too, so I couldn't blame him much, but I scrambled for a different entry point.

"That, sure. Or spirituality. Or maybe even the supernatural?"

Now he had stopped looking at the car and looked at me, his gaze scrutinizing. When I glanced sideways at him, I could see a small crease had appeared between his eyebrows and something was shining in his hazel eyes. Worry maybe? Caution? I rushed to try and smooth it over.

"I'm always curious," I said with a little shrug.

Rodney's shoulders relaxed, "I suppose so," he said after a moment. "I was raised Mormon, but I've never been as good of a follower as my dad wanted me to be."

Okay, now we were getting somewhere. "Is that because you believe in something different? Or...?" I let myself trail off. If he believed in anything not of this world, this conversation would be much easier. A strange feeling fluttered in my chest. It took me longer than it should have to realize it was hope.

He looked outside again as we came to the second bend, this one sharper, sending us both leaning in our seats. I chewed the inside of my cheek waiting for him to respond. *Come on, Rodney.* I wanted to snap at him like I had my first secretary. *Use your head!*

"I suppose I don't really believe in anything," he said finally, "not truly."

My heart sank at his words. *No, you have to be willing to* look. He would never believe me if that was the case. Which meant he would die, like all the others, and I would still be stuck in this god-forsaken loop all alone once more. This time had to be different. I wasn't going to *do* this anymore. It had to *end.*

"Really?" the word bubbled up my throat coated in exasperation. I couldn't help it. My heart jumped to a staccato beat as all those other deaths flashed before my eyes, the crunching and screaming playing in my head. If he didn't listen, he would end up just like them, and I would never break out of this. "If something supernatural was right in front of you, wouldn't you believe it?"

Rodney rolled his eyes "Well, there isn't anything supernatural in front of me, is there." It should have been a question, but the annoyance in his voice made it sound more like a fact.

I bit my lip, and a flush crept up my neck. When was the last time I felt a human touch? Or had a casual conversation that wasn't around trying to save the lives of the people who got caught in the same unfortunate cycle I was? God, I missed just sitting down and having a meal with another person. I missed trips on the boat and poker with friends. I'd never get the chance to do any of that again if someone didn't just listen to me. How was it *not even one* of these idiots could comprehend what I was saying?

I snorted, shaking my head. "I wouldn't be too sure of that."

Rodney's eyes flared wide, and I had seen fear enough to know what it looked like. But I couldn't stop now. Either he saw the pattern for himself, or I explained it to him. And I was convinced that telling him was the better way. I'd tried to see what would happen if I let others figure it out on their own. But it was never better. The results were always much worse.

He would listen to me whether he liked it or not.

I pushed the Thunderbird to go faster, preparing to point out the various points within the cycle as they came at us.

"What the hell does that mean?" he snapped, his hands balling into fists.

"Calm the fuck down and look," I snarled. "A raven is about to swoop towards the car. We'll miss it, don't worry."

Right on cue, a black feathered mass rushed past us, missing our windshield by inches as it squawked angrily. The first few cycles, that had scared the shit out of me. But you'd be surprised how quickly you get used to it.

Rodney flinched, just as I expected he might, "What the hell?!"

Pointing to the sign, *Heber 30 Miles,* coming up on our left I rushed to say, "I'm guessing you walked past that sign? Right?"

Rodney looked at it, his face pale as it fell back into my rearview mirror. I sped along the highway, shifting us up into sixth gear so the landmarks would come faster now. So he could see the cycle I needed him to see. The first bend was just up ahead, and as I took it, I could see him registering the familiarity of the movement as we both leaned through the sharp turn together.

"You're taking us in circles!" he snapped, his eyes wide and wild.

"No, Rodney," I said quickly, forcing my voice to drop lower even though I wanted to scream at him, "I'm not. *Look*. It's a loop." How many times had I said those lines? How many people had died on this god-forsaken road? I knew the exact number. It was thirty-seven. Well... thirty-eight if you counted all those years ago. Which I didn't.

"A creature is about to cross the road, a rabbit think." I paused. "Now!" I said as the furry blur shot from the tree line, thundering across the road through my headlights and safely to the other side. Rodney tracked the movement, but the slack jaw of his open mouth told me he still didn't believe it. He swallowed. I watched his Adam's apple bob once, twice, then a third time as his breathing came quicker.

Why wasn't he saying anything?

"I think it's a time loop," I pressed, rushing through the words as if speed would make them sink into Rodney's ears. "I've been stuck in it for a while. You have to believe me!" I expected him to argue, but no answer came from Rodney. When I glanced at him, he seemed frozen as his breath hitched to something wheezy. I wanted to scream at him to snap out of it, but I bit the inside of my cheek until I tasted the coppery tang of blood instead. As the boulders came into view, I pointed to them, "We passed those earlier, though... you might not remember them. You were looking at the car interior."

The only thing that ever changed about this damned continuous loop was the people on the side of the road. Yet, each one of them had died horrid deaths. Had they wandered into the loop I was currently stuck within? When they died, did they enter their own loop? Was that why I never saw them again? Or did their death doom me to another set of cycles, punishing me for my failure.

Not this time. Rodney was going to live.

"Stop it!" Rodney snapped, gripping his seat, his fingers leaving dimples in the leather.

But I roared us forward anyways so he could see the rest of the loop repeat itself again. If I got him to believe it, maybe we could get out together. Maybe I could go back to my life where I had status and money and a corner office and people who respected me.

"It's just around the bend," I assured him. My hands clutched the steering wheel so hard it groaned under the pressure. My stomach lurched sideways as we whipped around the second bend. Surely, when he saw the sign for a third time, everything would click. He would realize what I meant by a time loop. And if he realized, if he believed me, it might be enough to break the loop all together.

Rodney was pushing himself away from me, trying, and failing, to make his large lanky body shrink into the passenger seat. His gaze flicked from me to the road and back again as the raven surged forward, once more barely missing my windshield with an angry caw. At the sight of it, Rodneys breath hitched, coming in short gasps.

"Calm down, Rodney," I ordered. We were almost to the sign, going so fast that the trees surrounding the road rushed past us in a blur. "Look!" I said pointing as my headlights illuminated the weather-worn wood just enough for us to see the outline. "It's the same sign!"

Heber 30 Miles

He saw the pattern now; the recognition in his eyes was undeniable. But my throat constricted as I noted a wild look as well. Panic, pure animal panic. *No, no, no! Not again!* I had seen that look before. I knew what would come next. He didn't believe it. He still thought I was taking him in circles, like I was some serial killer set out to confuse him. He would try to escape me. And when he did... he would die.

"It's okay, Rodney," I said, my own voice coming out broken and desperate as I still tried to stop the enviable. "Please...you can't freak out." I reached out towards him, trying to assure him.

The move was a mistake. It seemed to snap Rodney out of his delirium.

"Let me out! Let me the FUCK OUT!" He began yanking at the door handle, scrambling to find the locking mechanism so he could launch himself from the car. I grabbed a fistful of Rodney's coat, tugging him towards me as his fingers scratched against the door. The Thunderbird veered dangerously as the movement yanked the steering wheel.

"Rodney, stop! You can't go out there. It's not safe!"

Not again. Not again. Why is this happening to me?

He had to understand. He had to *live*. I didn't think I could hear the screaming and crunching of yet another person I had failed to save. But his scrambling fingers found the lock, and he threw the door open, letting in a burst of cold rushing air. I slammed on the brakes, and we screeched to a stop as I grabbed at his arm like an anchor.

"Listen to me. Just LISTEN," I yelled. "It's a cycle. It repeats itself, but if you stay in the car, you are safe!" At least I hoped so. They always died outside the car.

"Get the fuck off of me you crazy asshole!" he snapped, trying to tear free of my vise-like grip. His free hand snapped forward, his closed fist smashing into my jaw with brutal force.

I reeled back, losing my grip on his arm as my vision blurred. His hit knocked my grip loose and blurred my vision, but I still clawed at him frantically, the fabric of his coat slipping through my fingers as he ripped out of the car.

"Leave me the hell alone, Frank!" he spat, slamming the door closed.

No, no, no! Just like all the others, he didn't believe me. The loop wasn't going to end. He was going to die, and I'd be alone again. "Wait! Rodney, *PLEASE!*" I screamed after him so loudly it felt like my throat was ripping open. "COME BACK!"

Rodney ignored me, his feet pounding as he ran down the road away from my car, fast enough I could see his arms pumping in my rearview mirror. But then a bright light blinded me, and I knew it was too late.

I closed my eyes and put my hands over my ears, ignoring the pain in my jaw as I tried to shut it out. But it wasn't enough to block the horrid high-pitched screech of brakes locking up. The crunching of bones crashing against metal. Rodney screaming, surprised and loud at first, then dropping into a keening wail. Though I tried to block the sound out with my hands, it made no difference.

I had failed. I had truly and utterly failed Rodney, but what was worse was that I had failed all of them. Martha. Dan. Greg. Stephanie. Molly. And so many more. Was this loop my hell? What had I done to deserve this? To witness the horrific sounds of their deaths over and over again as I lingered behind. Stuck only with memories of them and the lonely road ahead.

Rodney's keening had turned into a garbled whine, and I dared to look in the rearview window once more. His body was twisted at odd angles, his right leg a few feet from him, the remaining stump gushing blood out onto the asphalt. His head completely twisted around, chin resting against his back shoulder blade as he choked and gagged. My Thunderbird's taillights illuminating his face in an angry red light as his desperate eyes searched for help.

I started to sob then. My tears blurred his twisted expression in my rearview mirror. He looked so much like the man from that night. The one whose name I would never know. Who I'd driven away from before he'd grown cold. For a long time, the only thing I could hear was my sobbing and Rodney's gargled gasping, until we both went silent.

Daring to check in the rear-view mirror again, I found Rodney unmoving, his eyes wide open and staring at the dark clouds above. The Thunderbird's engine hummed beneath me, steady and unbothered by the horror it had just witnessed. Ahead, the dark road was illuminated by my headlights. The only way ahead. And the only way away from the twisted body behind me.

So, I shifted the car into drive, slowly, laboriously, like cattle prodded to move forward. Just like the others, he would be gone by the time I reached this spot again in the loop. Had he ever even existed? Or was he a horrible figment of the loop sent to torture me? Perhaps, the next person I saw, I should just leave on the side of the road. Maybe they wouldn't die if I did.

Yet, one hundred and twenty-three cycles later, I couldn't help myself when I spotted a woman carrying a heavy bag waving at me from the side of the highway. Maybe this time, I could convince her. Maybe this time I'd finally break the loop.

As I came to a stop, I cleared my raw throat and forced a smile, "Need a lift?"

The North Country

Arthur Petersen

A cross fields wintered creatures croak.
Glad journey e'en though you impugn,
And sully with outlandish joke:
'Her cauldron blots out stars and moon
'By seething out such vapor, smoke!'

'Round yawning mouth that boils to brim,
'It sings for miles down ev'ry path:
'A call to gently touch the rim.
'To join their flesh in broth and bath,
'To clamber up and dive within?'

Then gust breach garments sharp as darts,
And like a wound her form appears,
Her ladle draws sinew apart.
Her warty lip drinks up their ears;
She hoists aloft the melting heart.

I say I'm wrong, for what it's worth...
A curse replete with awful gloom,
Detaches us from all our mirth:
She'll seize the shadow from the moon,
She'll place it down upon the earth.

While we yet have time...
We'll wallow in love on the road,
In the wind of the North Country.
We'll locate the sorrow all shall know;
Her cackle will find its way to me.

Driving Angry Opens Doors

Steve Capone, Jr.

The night I disappeared, I was driving off my latest argument with Ryker, my eternally bratty fourteen-year-old. Remember that line in *Groundhog Day*, "Don't drive angry"? An aphorism for life, that. But driving had always calmed me, so I figured that night would be the same as all the others. That drive was different, and I'll tell it like it happened—maybe my wait will be cut short if I learn something. Probably not, though.

The roads jutting off the old Pony Express route are few and far between, many of them appearing on no maps but the most detailed backcountry guides, and I couldn't tell you if they've got names. This lack stands in direct spite of my having explored the nooks, crannies, and cornices of canyons and open desert alike damn near every weekend since I bought my truck, on which the sales guy must've known my name was written in blood the moment I stepped onto that cursed lot. You know what I've found? Most of them are closed circuits, just like the wider world is a closed loop. But these roads are calm and unoccupied circuits, good for driving.

Oh, how that old truck opened doors for me, boy howdy. Ryker's mother never would have let me run so wild. Something about being able to pound every surface on land without much fear of capsizing my landship—knowing I could roam wherever I wanted—knowledge of this truth changed me, made me whole again. I'd think it, and then—poof!—I'd disappear in a cloud of all-terrain-tire dust.

I should hurry up this entry—I can't know how much time I have left before the arrival, and I don't want to be inside for it. I think I need to be there. Who knew what'd happen were I to miss it?

To go out Pony Express is to tread into the desert, just as to tread up Skyline Drive is to climb a mountain, far from the city and its California transplants with all their goddamned money. Any escape from the smog and human pollution is worthy of a bit of effort. But I'm getting off track here. The point is context. I was mad at Ryker, knowing I played some part in our latest blowup but knowing they were just as much, if not more, to blame. I'd driven into the desert to be alone a hundred or two hundred other times. It wasn't always about my kid, but something always ticked me off—shitty Utah drivers cutting me off or driving fifteen under the speed limit in the left-hand lane, a neighbor refusing to acknowledge my goddamned friendly wave, some idiot leaving their shopping cart in the middle of the lot derelict and a danger to every vehicle in the place. It was always something, and while driving angry might be a bad idea where there are other cars on the road, there were no other cars out in the desert.

What I hadn't done a hundred times was to stay out there by myself overnight. I'd camped all over the state of Utah, but not without gear, not without water, and not without letting someone know where I was getting off to. Ryker needed me, despite their shitty, entitled attitude. You don't just go into the backcountry alone and hope nothing goes wrong. You plan for the worst-case scenario, let people know where your body might be discovered if you don't check back in twelve or twenty-four hours later, and you take water and gasoline sufficient for three times what you need. I don't prep this way for my cool-down drives; this night was no different. I would drive in silence until I felt better, pick a turnaround spot, get out and meditate for a few breaths, and then return home. All would be well.

The West Desert is a vast space rippled with north-south mountain ranges, with flats between the ripples I'd liken to ventricles which, standing in place, you can see for just about forever in at least two directions. These're some of the flattest valleys on the planet, and Pony Express Road stabs west out of the populated Wasatch Front into the heart of this glorious nothing, with dirt trails leading northward and southward like capillaries. If you should take this road away from society and just go out, *out, out* into the empty, you're unlikely to meet many others along your way, whether you're out there for two hours or two days. And if you traipse along one of those northbound or southbound capillaries, you'll not spot another human soul. And seeing as being on my lonesome was my goal after the latest blowout with Ry, I picked one of these venules at random and followed it off Pony Express.

Now you've got the context, or as much of it as I understood, for the evening's events.

So, there I was, maybe about 11:30 at night under an unobtrusive new moon, doing about 18 mph along a rutted northerly trail. I cruised under a patternless miasma of stars, a blanket thick enough to be unrecognizable. I'd flipped off my headlights and doused the dashboard lights so my eyes would adjust to the moonlit landscape and starlit skyscape. The desert positively glowed under starlight. It was flat as hell out there—near enough to the spot where they do those world speed records. Every now and again, a low hill would appear and hide the curved horizon, the barrier line between glowing land and galaxies many lifetimes away.

Steering with care, I mostly stared at the horizon for some forty minutes of driving from the main road. The heart med my doc prescribed as an alternative to a benzodiazepine was doing its subtle magic, and I was beginning to forget my kid's piss-poor attitude.

I picked the crest of the next low hill as my turnaround. I'd step out of the truck for a long look around, take in the nothingness the desert offered, and then hop back in and double back toward home.

Standing on the slight rise, I spotted a low star—at ground level—distinct from the foreign skies above. Incandescent and flickering, this was no dirt bike or headlamp LED, nor the ditch lights of another off-highway rig. I wondered. A lantern, maybe? Did someone need help? I drove toward it. How could I not have done so?

I plodded my slow path toward the light. I seemed to be getting closer, but—does this make sense?—not in proportion to how far it seemed I'd driven.

I'd been reading this book just around then, *Lost Signals*, and in that collection was a story about a guy driving along an empty road not unlike the one I was trundling along at that moment, and I'd be lying if I said I wasn't thinking about it just then. In that story, the driver hears an odd message from a kind of ghost radio station and follows the signal to its source. I don't remember how that one ended. It was a good story but discomforting.

I kept an eye on the fuel gauge. I'm not new.

I tracked the light further north. Gradually, it resolved into a yellowed bulb fixed over a door. Now almost upon it, I could tell it was just that, too. A door in the desert, a bit of framing, and nothing but open space behind it. I remember thinking, "Now what in creation is this?" It was a question born of curiosity, not of fear.

I parked the truck, switched on the ambers and high beams, and climbed down. I didn't see any signs warning away trespassers or intruders, but I knew there was no guarantee there weren't any. And I've read enough spooky stuff to know running right up, turning the handle, and investigating what the door protected was a grade-A way of terminating this drive. But I was compelled. It was weird, right? So, I approached with caution, maintaining a twenty-foot bubble, and edging around it in a broad circle.

Turns out, I'd been mistaken at first impression. It was more than a door and its frame—but not much more. This was an entry to a storm cellar or underground bunker or whatever you'd want to call it. Stretching from the backside of the door angled toward the ground was the roof of a stairwell. Standing behind the door and its tunnel had me thinking of giant Australian trapdoor spiders or passages to otherworldly circuits.

It'd be better to explore, if I would choose to do so at all, during the day. Daylight has a knack for showing phenomena previously thought odd aren't so strange after all. Back at my truck, I leaned into the driver's side doorway and grabbed the gridded *Utah Off-Road* book. I began triangulating between the spot where I think I'd left Pony Express, I-80 to the north, and the mountain ranges to my east and west. I found what I suspected to be the line of my little road cutting across pages somewhere in the middle of the atlas.

Something at the edge of my vision caught my attention. The man standing in front of my truck and squinting into my ditch lights nearly frightened me into my grave. If only. But this is just a figure of speech.

The man stood stock still and held an old cowboy hat in front of his face with one hand. He'd fixed his other hand out in front of him as though blocking the LED rays nearly blasting through him enough to show up in a pattern of red gelatin relief on the door behind him. I felt safe in part because he didn't hold a firearm, as I might reasonably have expected while meeting a stranger out in the desert.

He called out. "Been waiting for you, hoss!" His voice was gravelly, presumably a consequence of a lifetime's worth of desert dust in the lobes of those lungs.

"How?" I wondered but didn't say, my own voice removed from my sternum.

He answered anyway. "Could see you comin' a long way off." He gestured toward Pony Express. "Must've been twenty minutes or more since you turned north." He paused. "Saw my light, I take it?"

I said nothing. Twenty minutes? I'd been on the northbound trail for two hours, easy.

"You must be a little confused, pal of mine." He coughed and spat. "Don't you worry overmuch about it. Out here, time stretches out—turns elastic, you might say. Pulls tighter and loosens up. It breathes." He surveyed the landscape around him and then continued. "It's that kind of place. Truth be told, maybe I got it wrong a minute ago. You could've been headed this way for three straight days, and I mightn't have known the difference. Come to think of it, what day did you leave town?"

That much I felt comfortable answering. "It's the twenty-second."

"Don't presume. I asked what day you left town—not for the here and now."

"Uh, the twenty-second?"

"Of?"

"June?" I was confused, I'd have admitted. I suppose maybe this guy didn't have a calendar in his bunker or whatever it was, but—

He interrupted my thoughts. "Year?"

What the hell? Was this a Kyle Reese *Terminator* reference? He was joking. I waited for him to crack a smile or chuckle at the city-slicker falling for his ruse... but none came. I asked, "What do you do out here? Something to do with Dugway? You an Army outfit?"

He shook his head. "No Army around here. Observatory."

Observatory? I leaned, clearly searching for the telltale sign I must have missed, a telescope or something indicating this space counted as the thing he'd named. "An observatory?"

"Yup." He adjusted his hands to block more of the lights from my truck. "Partner, would you mind..." He motioned at the truck.

If I was in for a penny, I was surely in for a pound, and in the half-moment I weighed whether or not to do what he'd wanted. I regarded him with some care. Once I got involved with whatever this was, I'd follow it through. But I'd already made my choice, back at that bluff. Back home when I told Ryker where he could put his opinion about how I talked about the neighbors.

I took in this man's appearance. Jeans and a flannel. Cowboy hat in hand. He hadn't shaved in a few days, but he was no stranded soldier. His face was full enough I didn't figure him to be sizing me up as a few meals' worth of "special meat" like the cannibals in *Tender is the Flesh*. I switched off the ditch lights. My eyes adjusted. We both blinked at each other.

"Look, pal, I'll explain, and I'm not going to do you any harm. I'm just glad you're finally here."

Who says that? I was intensely curious, though. I shook his hand. Does it strike you as strange I don't remember what I said to him or what he said to me when we shook hands? We must have introduced ourselves then.

"What do you need?" I asked him as I followed him toward the door.

"Just another pair of eyes to have a look at something."

"At what?"

"I told you we were an observatory, right?"

"Well, I'm no astronomer. I can't even find the Big Dipper."

He grinned. "We're not that kind of observatory, friend." He turned and opened the door behind him, waiting for me there.

I locked the truck and pocketed the keys.

The observer led the way inside and down a set of metal-grate stairs.

I paused at the top. Incandescents like the one outside hummed overhead, strung up in regular intervals. Our shoes clanked against the metal and echoed down the angular trachea until we reached a lacquered concrete floor. The temperature dropped as we hit the ground probably forty feet underneath the desert floor. I shivered.

The observer didn't look at me but said, "Always a brisk fifty-five down here. No need for heating or air conditioning. Nature's way." He hung his hat beside the entry and kicked off his shoes, placing them on a folded Navajo rug. "Mind?" He indicated my own.

I took in the scene. It struck me as something like an old missile silo, except stretched out instead of conical, maybe more like the space station from *Event Horizon*. True enough, a kitchen-living room-bedroom economy flat that would have been at home in *Alien* lay in front of me, all metal and concrete except for purpose-made soft spaces like a sofa and a bunk for one.

"Please empty your pockets. The instrumentation doesn't like the interference of remotes and phones and such."

I hadn't told Ryker where I was. I never did, of course. I got home when I got home, and I had always come home before.

Keys in the basket?

Oh, no. I knew what this was. We were about to cross into some side room where the observers got the collected wallets and keys of every poor sod who's come out here over the last twenty years. That's the reveal.

I didn't think so, though, somehow. I emptied my pockets.

There was a side door to this room, and the observer headed for it. I waited to see what would happen when he opened it. Inside the door were computer banks.

"This is some NSA shit" was my thought just then.

Again, I hadn't spoken aloud, but the observer answered anyhow. "Not NSA, Brandon."

Had I given him my name?

I followed him into a corridor between columned server racks. Maybe fifteen feet into the room, things opened up. Monitors—two dozen of them—played out what looked like real-time videos of... of me. Of me, but not of *me*. It's almost impossible to describe this should've-been-impossible thing. One screen showed a much older me sitting in a McDonald's booth by myself, drinking coffee and holding a book. My eyes watered on screen as they watered where I stood. Another caught me stepping out of the shower, just a waif of a man—my age—but this wasn't the me I know. A third had me and a woman I didn't recognize smiling at each other without speaking, like we'd known each other for ages. This version of me couldn't have been more than a couple of years older than I was as I stood there, rooted in my core to the concrete underfoot.

But I had no woman in my life. Not since Ryker's mother. And I couldn't imagine there ever being another. No one would take her place—not for either of us.

The man stepped to the side and may as well have disappeared as I continued scanning the monitors.

I found and fixated on a version looking exactly as I saw myself that day—at age thirty-nine—with a hint of the same tattoo peeking from under a shirt matching one I wore at that moment.

My perception closed to a funnel, and the other scenes on all the other monitors disappeared as I watched myself tell my child they were selfish, ought to consider all I'd done for them, and snapped that maybe we should just keep to ourselves for a few days. The screen shifted then into a first-person perspective, as though a camera were looking out from this me's interior, and the tears welling in Ryker's eyes were just as I'd seen them what I still thought of as mere hours earlier. I felt the same fury as the character on screen. This image shifted again into a close third, and it followed me as I grabbed my keys, stepped outside, and disappeared off screen.

That was what had happened, to the finest detail.

What it showed next wasn't in my own memories because, at that point, I was in my truck, breathing myself into calmness sufficient to allow me arrive safely at Pony Express fourteen miles to the southwest of our townhome in a new exurb of Salt Lake City. In the video, Ryker is standing in the living room looking out the of oversized front windows at the truck. Their fists are clenched, as they'd been when I'd left. They screamed then, and it echoed not fury but comprised every helpless and hopeless feeling I'd ever had since we'd found Ryker's mother—Whitney, I forced myself to say her name in my mind and maybe aloud—in bed that Thursday afternoon in 2014. Fuck Thursdays. Their cry was an agony I understood but about which we'd never spoken.

And then I watched as Ryker disappeared into their room. I exhaled.

But the scene didn't cut out there or shift to me in the truck.

The camera followed as though held by a Steadicam operator. Ryker fell onto their bed for a moment and then, as though stumbling into a wholly novel idea, reached beneath the mattress and box spring and came out with something. Something small enough to fit in their hand. It stabbed out one end of their closed fist, a fist safer and softer than what it had been in the living room or kitchen moments before. Ryker placed whatever this was beside them on the bed, but the camera didn't have the right angle, and they shoved their hand behind their headboard and extracted something else. They then exhaled heavily as they sat, not uncomfortable but not overly comfortable, either—taking a position to attend to something rather than to have a good cry, burying oneself in pillows and blankets. A lighter. That is the first thing I see. Ryker reaches back to the first thing they'd grabbed. A bag. Small. A gram baggie. A metal measuring cup from the kitchen. What the fuck? I watched Ryker pour the contents of this bag into the tiny cup and dribble water from their bottle in on top... I would say that I froze, but this is clearly the wrong way to describe it. Everything in me was alive at that moment. I felt the vasculature of my entire circulatory system explode with highly oxygenated blood, my brain a multiplicating fission of adrenaline for fuel. But I stayed where I was. I couldn't not watch. Ryker tied off and inserted the needle, and my eyes hurt from how widely my body had forced them open. "No," I think I said. Ryker's eyes fluttered, and they slumped over.

Then, nothing. The camera held. A shadow fell across my child's body.

"Wake up," I commanded the person on the screen.

There was no movement.

"Wake up." My breath hitched. For all the oxygen my body had pumped into my muscles, I couldn't breathe at that moment. "No. Please. Wake up." I nearly collapsed just then before realizing that if I could get back to Ryker, maybe I could stop this. Or maybe it was another Ryker—not mine and Whitney's darling child. I turned, and my face must have said everything.

"You know which of these moving images is your story. You always do."

"But Ryker..."

"The very worst of all possible worlds. Your world."

At that moment, I wished he'd had a firearm. I'd have wrestled him, thrashed the older man, clawed his fucking eyes out of his head to get hold of it. I'd have shot myself without hesitation.

The observer shook his head.

"I can't," I said then.

"You don't have to go back."

I looked at him, the numbness now leaving my cheeks, which were again feeling wet.

"There's a room for you down the other side."

I squinted and looked where he pointed. Another door, just like the one we'd entered.

"I'm thinking you can help me," he said.

I said nothing.

"There has to be a way—" At this, his voice caught in his throat. "We can stop it. We can stop hers, too." He gestures to a viewscreen at the far left of the bank of screens.

And there she was. Ryker's mother. My love. My everything. Her long brown hair pulled back like she did when she cooked. She sliced a tomato, its redness pooling under her deft fingers. She looked back at the camera. It was her. My Whitney. But this was not a day I remembered, and I was pretty sure I remembered every instant with her. I'd worked at it like a prisoner building a mansion in his mind, brick by brick, trying with every sober moment I allowed myself to reconstruct our eleven years together, one moment at a time. The human memory is a magical, terrible thing.

"But why... why stay?" I asked.

"Every few weeks or months or years, another version of you—of me—comes along. I try to play 'weird desert mystic guy' as best I can and guide him to be wiser, calmer, more loving, and patient and kind. I send him back into the world. A world, anyway. We don't always get here by way of anger and loss, you know?"

I nod. I can't go back.

"What about my truck?" It's such a stupid thing, but it was my thought right then. Where would I park it so it wouldn't fall apart from high desert winds sandblasting it to hell?

"It's already gone," the observer replies. "I don't understand how it works, but we close that door, and... a new circuit."

I nod.

He waves me toward the door we hadn't yet been through.

Another efficiency apartment like his own.

He pulled open the underbunk drawer. Jeans and tee shirts. He gestured to a stairwell, and beside it hung a cowboy hat like his.

I looked back toward the room with the computers. "I have to see..."

He nodded. "I understand. It's the same for me. We don't want to miss anything, right? Any detail that might have us say the right thing, to undo what we've done, what the world has done." He smiled just then. "I told you I need your help. A second pair of eyes."

"There are a lot of monitors in there," I said, marching past him toward the screens.

Two pairs of eyes are better than one.

"We'll work together," I said.

"Together," the observer answered.

About the Authors

Eric John Anderson (He/Him) is an award-winning author and screenwriter from Utah. He has lived on both American coasts, but finds peace when lost deep in the mountain wilderness or going thrift shopping with his husband. When he's not writing queer literary fiction or supernatural horror, he's playing intense strategy board games or describing obscure films to uninterested friends. His work can be found in *Utah's Best Poetry & Prose 2025* and the upcoming anthology *Twisted Tales*.

Brian B. Baker is a horror writer and reviewer. You can find his book reviews on Substack at https://substack.com/@brianbbaker. He lives in northern Utah with his wife, kids, and the family dog. You can find other published books anywhere books are sold.

Founder and editor-in-chief of Whisper House Press, whose *Costs of Living* and *Dread Mondays* horror anthologies release in the fall of 2025, **Steve Capone, Jr.** is an HWA member and award-winning Utah-based prose author and screenwriter hailing from the Rust Belt. Find him via his incorporeal footprint at https://linktr.ee/steve-caponejr.

Travis Coleman was born and raised in Cache Valley Utah. He still lives there with his wife, two children, and a various assortment of random critters. In his spare time he dreams of writing really cool books, he just needs to stop getting distracted by shiny things.

Lawrence Dagstine is a native New Yorker and speculative fiction writer of 30 years. He has placed over 500+ short stories in online and print periodicals during that period of time. He has been published by houses such as Damnation Books, Steampunk Tales, Wicked Shadow Press, Black Beacon Books, Farthest Star Publishing, Calliope Interactive, and Dark Owl Publishing (with which he has a new book out called *The Nightmare Cycle*). Visit his website, for publication history past and present, at: www.lawrencedagstine.com

James Fritz graduated from Loyola University Chicago with degrees in business and music. He recently quit his job as a data analyst to write full-time. He enjoys reading and writing, piano, jiu jitsu, snuggling with his wife, and his self-appointed role as president of the Evgeny Kissin fan club. Several of his short stories have been picked up by publishers such as Gypsum Sound Tales, Hellbound Books, and Black Hare Press. You can find him on Instagram under the handle @jame s.fritz.writing.

https://linktr.ee/james.fritz.writing

C. H. Lindsay (Charlie) is an award-winning poet & writer, house-wife, and book-lover—not necessarily in that order. She currently has short stories and poems in over forty anthologies and magazines including *Amazing Stories, Fantasy Magazine, Moonletters, Space and Time Magazine, Strange Horizons,* and *Utah's Best Poetry and Prose.* She is currently working on five novels, six short stories, and at least two dozen poems (although the numbers are always in flux).

In 2018 she became Al Carlisle's literary executor. She now publishes his true crime under *Carlisle Legacy Books, LLC*.

She is a member of SFWA, HWA, SFPA, LUW, and is a founding member of the Utah Chapter of the Horror Writers Association. Mostly blind, she lives in Utah with her "seeing-eye husband," library of books, and a bossy cat. You can learn more about her at www.chlindsay.net.

Emily Harney has been writing since childhood, having her poetry published at the age of 14. She is now self-published author with her first novella, *The Woman In The Woods* released in 2022. She also has a blog of short horror stories at her website, shorttalestallstories.com.

Danielle Harward is a professional ghostwriter who writes fantasy and horror in her personal time. Her short stories have won several awards and have been published in over ten anthologies. She loves to paint, shoot arrows, and chat about her bird. And as someone who typically writes over 50,000 words a month, some wonder if she is clinically insane.

Juleigh Howard-Hobson's poetry has appeared in *Amazing Stories*, *The Dead Lands*, *Midnight Echo*, *The Audient Void*, *Dreams and Nightmares*, *Under Her Skin* (Black Spot) *Vastarien: Women's Horror* (Grimscribe), and many other places. Nominations include the Pushcart, Elgin, Best of the Net and Rhysling. Her latest book is *Curses, Black Spells and Hexes* (Alien Buddha). An active member of both the SFPA and the HWA, she lives in a suitably haunted house on the edge of the known world. Bluesky: @juleigh.bsky.social / X: @poetforest

David McLachlan is a disabled veteran author who lives and works in Northern California. His stories and poems have been published or are forthcoming in various magazines. You can connect with him at DavidMcLachlanWriter.com or on Bluesky: @davidmclachlan.bs ky.social.

LEHUA PARKER wanted to climb pyramids and translate hieroglyphics until she discovered that was prime zombie territory. Since eating brains was definitely not her jam, she pivoted to creating the kinds of stories for kids and adults that she wished she could have found in her school libraries.

Much of Lehua's award-winning writing is deeply embedded in Hawaiian island culture, including the Niuhi Shark Saga trilogy, a magical realism series about two brothers, one a surfing star and the other allergic to water. Her irreverent speculative short stories can be found in a plethora of publications including *Va: Stories by Women of the Mona, Bamboo Ridge, Dialogue, An Ocean of Wonder,* and *Fua,* and are collected in *Sharks in an Inland Sea.*

Now living in exile in the high Rocky Mountains far from her island home, during snowy winter months she dreams of the beach. Connect with her at www.LehuaParker.com.

Cygnus Perry is an undergraduate student at Utah State University. They have lived in Utah since they were in high school where they developed a passion for creative writing. Cygnus loves to explore the natural world and uses it as inspiration for unnatural stories and poems. For Cygnus, writing is the best way to discover the unreal and unbelievable.

https://www.instagram.com/perrypurplefingers/
https://twitter.com/PerryPianist

Arthur Petersen works for tabletop game publisher *Petersen Games*. When he's not doing that, or spending time with his five daughters, he writes fiction and music. Follow Arthur at: existoid.com

Melissa Pierce is a lifelong writer and novelist, though Burial of Broken Vows is her first published work. Her chaotic (yet visually satisfying) sticky note system for storyboarding novels has been documented on her TikTok channel, @melwritestoomuch, to over 70,000 followers. She can be contacted at https://melissagottula.wixsite.com/writes.

Jonathan Reddoch is co-owner of Collective Tales Publishing. He is a father, writer, editor, and publisher. He writes sci-fi, fantasy, romance, and especially horror. He focuses primarily on flash fiction, but also writes poetry and short stories. He has been working on his enormous sci-fi novel for over a decade and would like to finish it in this lifetime if possible. He's from southern California but lives in Salt Lake City. Find him on Instagram: @Allusions_of_Grandeur_ CTPfiction.com

Jay Seate stands on the side of the literary highway and thumbs down whatever genre comes roaring by. His storytelling runs the gamut from Horror Novel Review's Best Short Fiction to the *Chicken Soup for the Soul* series. His fiction incorporates fantasy, suspense, or humor featuring the quirkiest of characters. His latest eclectic collection, *Gallery of Souls*, by J. Troy Seate is available at Amazon.

Adrian Speth (he/they) is a trans and queer artist consistently on the road but currently in Boston. Originally raised in a rural Utah town, his work often explores the horror of isolation, liminality, and loss of community. Most recently, his work has appeared in Third Estate Books' *Spectrum: An Autistic Horror Anthology*, Sundress Publications' *Transmasculine Poetics*, and his play *Jesus On Ice* was produced for Boston University's 2024 STAMP season.

Elizabeth Suggs is the co-owner of the indie publisher Collective Tales Publishing, owner of Editing Mee, and is the author of a growing number of award-winning published stories, one of which titled "Into the Dark" part of the *Collective Darkness* anthology was Amazon Bestseller and another was selected for second place in the Quills Short Story Contest "Technicolor Tears." She is also a book reviewer (EditingMee.com), popular bookstagrammer, and cosplayer (@ElizabethSuggsAuthor). When she's not writing or reading, she's traveling the world or doing yoga.

G.D. Watry is a writer from California. His fiction and poetry have been published in *Like The Wind Magazine, Pantheon Magazine, OCCULUM,* and *Hinnom Magazine,* among other publications.

Johnny Worthen is a widely published, award-winning, best-selling author of books and stories. Trained in stand-up comedy, modern literary criticism and cultural studies, he writes excellent multi-genre fiction, symbolized by his love of tie-dye and good words. "I wear tie-dye for my friends, but I write what I like to read," he says. "This guarantees me at least one fan and easy dressing decisions in the morning." Johnny teaches writing at the University of Utah and lives in a house with his wife, assorted cats. There's also a lawn. Find him at: www.johnnyworthen.com.

Bryan Young (he/they) works across many different media. His work in film has been called "filmmaking gold" by *The New York Times*. He's published comic books with Slave Labor Graphics and Image Comics and is co-writing the upcoming BattleTech series of graphic novels with New York Times Bestseller Michael A. Stackpole. He's been a regular contributor for the Huffington Post, StarWars .com, Star Wars Insider magazine, SYFY, /Film, and more. In 2014, he wrote the critically acclaimed history book, *A Children's Illustrated History of Presidential Assassination*. He co-authored *Robotech: The Macross Saga RPG* and its companion *Homefront* and has written six books in the BattleTech Universe. His latest non-fiction tie-in book, *The Big Bang Theory Book of Lists* is a #1 Bestseller on Amazon. His work has won two Diamond Quill awards and in 2023 he was named Writer of the Year by the League of Utah Writers. He teaches writing for *Writer's Digest, Script Magazine,* and at the University of Utah. Follow him across social media @swankmotron or visit swankmotron.com.

A Note from Timber Ghost Press

If you enjoyed *No Exit*, please consider leaving a review on Amazon or Goodreads. Reviews help the authors and the press.

If you go to www.timberghostpress.com you can sign up for our newsletter so you can stay up-to-date on all our upcoming titles, plus you'll get informed of new horror flash fiction and poetry featured on our site monthly.

Take care and thanks for reading *No Exit!*

-Timber Ghost Press